THE FIXER

A DARK BRATVA ROMANCE

RENEE ROSE

D1596549

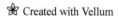

WANT FREE RENEE ROSE BOOKS?

Go to http://subscribepage.com/alphastemp to sign up for Renee Rose's newsletter and receive a free copy of *Alpha's Temptation*, *Theirs to Protect*, *Owned by the Marine*, *Theirs to Punish*, *The Alpha's Punishment*, *Disobedience at the Dressmaker's* and *Her Billionaire Boss*. In addition to the free stories, you will also get bonus epilogues, special pricing, exclusive previews and news of new releases.

CHAPTER 1

MY FATHER'S men say he only has days to live. Maybe only hours. We're at his home in Moscow—a residence I've never been permitted to enter before.

A place I hated from the time I was a little girl.

It means little to me now. Ditto on his approaching death.

I can't say I love the man. He was a terrible father and a worse partner to my mother. Partner, not husband—no, he couldn't marry her.

It's against the bratva code.

She was his kept mistress for thirty years until last week when he informed her she was now the mistress of Vladimir, his right-hand man. That's right—he literally bestowed his mistress on another man. Like she was some whore he owned. No, worse than a whore—like she was his slave.

She had no choice in the matter.

Like I say, he's not a nice man, my father.

"Come, Sasha, your father wants to see you," my mother says in a hushed tone. My once beautiful mother suddenly appears old. She's pale, her face drawn up and pinched in grief.

Despite it all, she still loves my father deeply.

I follow her into his room. He didn't want to die in a hospital, so his large bedroom has been converted to one. Medical machines surround him; there are nurses on duty twenty-four/seven. The curtains are open, letting the summer sun in through the large windows.

"Aleksandra." He calls me by my full name.

I flinch. He's still as formidable as ever, even thin and frail in his crimson striped robe. His face is a deathly grey pallor.

"Come." He summons me to his side. I walk over reluctantly. I may be twenty-three, but something about the man makes me still feel like an errant child. He takes my hand, and I have to work not to shudder at the feel of his dry, bony fingers holding mine.

"Sasha, I will provide for you," he says. Coughs.

I swallow.

Providing for us was the only good thing he did for me and my mother. I should be grateful. We've lived in luxury for our whole lives. I even got to attend the college of my choice in the United States—University of Southern California, where I studied acting. But of course, he summoned me back the moment I graduated.

And I came because he holds the purse-strings.

If he leaves me enough money in his will, I plan to go back to America to pursue my dreams.

"Your husband arrives today."

I don't even understand his words at first. I blink. Look over my shoulder at my mother. "Excuse me?" Surely I heard that wrong.

"The man who will marry you. To protect you and manage your financial interests."

I draw my hand back. "I'm sorry, *what?*"

Anger flickers on my father's face, and my body instantly responds with trembling. No matter how much I try not to care, I'm still the little girl just dying to please him, to win his love. To make him see me and give me attention this time.

Of course, I never show it. I've played the rebellious teenager with him for a long time now. I toss my hair for emphasis. "I am not marrying anybody."

He points a finger at me. "You will do what I tell you to do and be grateful I have found a way to protect and provide for you from the grave." A little spittle flies from his mouth.

My stomach churns. It's too disturbing to see death hammering his body and not to be affected, but I don't want to care. I want to just hate him through it all.

I do hate him.

"*Who?*" I demand. "Who am I to marry?"

A tap sounds on the door, and my father nods, like he's satisfied. Vladimir enters. "Maxim has arrived."

I lose my breath like I've been punched in the stomach.

Maxim.

Surely not? What kind of sick, twisted plan of my father's is this?

Maxim, the charming, powerful former protege of my father? The one I had exiled with my lies?

Maxim comes in, and I back away from my father toward the shadowed corner where my mother stands, hovering, wringing her hands. "You knew about this," I accuse.

Tears swim in her eyes. I'm glad because they help me swallow my own.

"Maxim." My father holds out his hand to him.

Maxim glances in our direction, and I make a move to leave, but my mother grabs my arm and keeps me in place. Vladimir, who also stepped into the room, shifts in front of the door like he's blocking it. Like he's a prison guard.

Nothing shows on Maxim's handsome face. Just the sight of him after six years makes my heart pound. He wears the same inscrutable mask I remember. Surely he hates me after what I did. He clasps my father's hand, going down on one knee beside the bed. "Papa."

Papa. That's what they call my father because he's their leader. In a way, I supposed he was like a father to Maxim, who I recall ran away from an orphanage at age fourteen. Probably a better father to him than he ever was to me, his real flesh and blood.

"At last, you've come," my father rasps, laying his free hand on Maxim's shoulder like a priest giving a benediction. "I have a dying request, Maxim."

"What is it?" Maxim's voice is low and respectful. Watching them, you'd never know my father banished Maxim, not only from his side but from this country.

"You have followed the Code of Thieves?"

Maxim nods.

"You have not taken a wife or family?"

"*Nyet.*"

"Good. You will break it now to marry Sasha," my father says.

Even though I half-expect it, the words still hit me like a tidal wave, crashing over me, washing me in panic.

Maxim's broad shoulders and back are to me, so I can't see his face, but he must be as horrified as I am.

He slowly rises from his kneeling position, slides his hands in his pockets and waits, not offering a response.

"I will leave my interest in all the oil wells to Sasha, only

4

so long as she is married to you. You will manage her financial interests and protect her from threats. If she dies before she bears children, the interest transfers to Vladimir, who is charged with leading the Moscow cell and caring for Galina, her mother."

"You're selling me," I choke from the corner.

He is—just like he sold my mother.

"*Silence!*" My father throws up a hand in my direction, not even deigning to look my way.

Maxim turns, though. He gives me a long, considering look, probably reminding himself how I ruined his life. He could have Vladimir's place at the helm of the bratva now if it hadn't been for me.

I press my lips together, so he won't see them tremble.

"She is not a virgin," my father says, like he's apologizing for delivering flawed goods.

I want to puke.

"She had a wild period out of my control when she went to college in America. But then, you are used to American women, no?"

Still, Maxim says nothing.

"You will do this for me," my father says. It's not a question, it's an order, but he watches Maxim's face intently, looking for clues. "Take her back to Chicago with you. Keep her out of the fray—protected and safe. Enjoy her money."

Maxim scrubs a hand over his face.

"You can punish her for the lie she told about you. No hard feelings, eh? You've done well for yourself in America. I hear Ravil lives like a king, and you enjoy the benefits."

I go still, hearing that my father knew I lied.

"And if I die first?" Maxim asks, all business. This is a transaction. My father's offering a dowry for my hand. "Who holds the interest in trust for Sasha?"

"Vladimir," my father says.

Maxim gives his head a small shake. Vladimir's in the room, but Maxim doesn't look his way. "Make it Ravil," he says. Ravil is the boss of the Chicago branch of bratva and Maxim's boss since his banishment.

My father considers, then looks at Vladimir. "Make the change," he orders. "And send in the clerk."

Vladimir immediately leaves the room.

"You will do this for me," my father repeats, looking at Maxim.

Maxim bows his head. "I will."

"Do not disrespect my name by disrespecting my daughter."

"Never," Maxim says immediately. He turns again and studies me. Something flutters in my lower belly at his dark gaze. If my father has his way, I will belong to this man. He will control me completely. My entire destiny is in his hands.

But I'm not going to lie down and play the submissive, doting, always available mistress my mother did.

Screw that.

I'm going to fight back.

~

Maxim

Fuck. Me.

There's no way I would refuse Igor his dying wish—or order, as the case may be. But this one is a fucking doozy.

I have to marry Sasha, his *mafiya* princess brat. The one who ruined my life. Not that I regret leaving Moscow. Igor's right—life is so much easier in Chicago under Ravil's rule. I don't constantly feel like a knife's about to go into my back the way I did here. But now I will again.

Of course, that's why he needs me to marry her.

Igor's oil well interests are worth at least sixty million. And his colleagues are unsavory, at best. We are the brotherhood of thieves, after all. So I have to presume at least thirty men will have their eyes on stealing that fortune in whatever way they can—killing Sasha, killing me, or even taking out the entire Chicago cell.

But I'm the fixer. Like Ravil, a master strategist, I have a reputation for outthinking my opponents. Igor knows his friends and enemies alike will think twice before they try to steal his fortune if it's in my care.

I take a good look at my unwilling, manipulative bride. She's even more beautiful than she was at seventeen, when I found her naked in my bed, set on seducing me.

She's drop-dead gorgeous, like her mother. Long, thick red hair. High cheekbones, porcelain skin. She has bright blue eyes and Cupid's bow lips. Her narrowed gaze is filled with hurt and rage.

Blyat. I will have my hands full with her.

Vladimir returns with the papers and a nervous-looking government official—I presume a clerk from the Department of Public Services. Someone probably paid or threatened him into making this a house-call instead of us going there.

If it were anyone besides Igor, I would demand to review his will to make sure the agreement is really as he states. But it's Igor, the man who literally saved my life, took me under his wing, and made me the man I am today. I'm not going to insult him. If his dying demand is that I marry his daughter, I'll do it.

Then again, Vladimir could be trying to fuck my bride out of her money, which is exactly the reason Igor inserted me into this mess. I keep my voice low and respectful. "Do you wish me to review it first, Papa?"

He considers me for a moment, then nods, so I take the sheaf of papers and skim through as quickly as I can. There are provisions for Galina, but all through Vladimir. Other than the oil interest, Igor's only legitimate business holdings, everything else goes to Vladimir, with strict provisions that he provides monthly allowance and protection to Galina.

The oil interest goes in a trust to Sasha, with me as trustee. We must remain married, or we forfeit the wells, and they go to Vladimir, or in his absence, Galina. If she dies first, Vladimir becomes the trustee. If I die first, Ravil. I nod and hand the papers to Igor to sign.

The clerk clears his throat and shifts on his feet.

"We're ready," I tell him.

Galina propels an angry Sasha forward to stand beside me. "This isn't happening," she complains in English, perhaps so her father won't understand. She's lucky she speaks it, or her new life would be even harder.

"Do you have rings to exchange?" the sweating clerk asks me.

"No." I shake my head.

Igor takes a platinum ring from his pinky finger. He's worn it for as long as I've known him. I remember him saying things to me like, "I, too, started with nothing, Maxim, and now I wear platinum rings."

His hand shakes when he hands it to me. His breathing is labored.

Galina notices and dashes to his side. "Are you all right, my love? Do you need more morphine?"

"Go on." Igor gives an impatient wave to the clerk. "Marry them."

The clerk swallows and launches into a brief ring

8

exchange. I put Igor's ring on Sasha's finger and tell the clerk to skip it when he comes to her ring for me.

"I now pronounce you husband and wife. You may kiss the bride."

I face Sasha, but she turns away, so I drop a kiss on her cheek. "It is done," I say to Igor.

"A-after you sign the certificate," the clerk stammers.

I snatch the pen from his hand and scrawl a quick semblance of my signature on the paper then hand the pen to Sasha.

Her fingers won't form around the pen. She looks up at me, rebellion swirling in those ocean blue eyes. As if either of us could stop this ball that's clearly been rolling long before we stepped in this room today.

"*Sign it*," Igor snaps. Or attempts to snap. It comes out as more of an angry wheeze.

Galina's mouth tightens. "Do it, Sasha."

Sasha grips the elegant fountain pen, the muscles around her jaw tightening as she signs the certificate.

The clerk signs it and nods at Vladimir. "It's complete. I'll have it filed in an hour." His hands tremble as he puts the certificate back in a folder, which he holds to his chest.

"Good. Bring the copies here, and you'll receive the rest of your payment."

The clerk exits like the room is on fire, and we all turn to Igor, whose breath has turned to a gasping.

"Get him morphine!" Galina barks at Vladimir, who calls in a nurse.

It's all too much to absorb. Igor dying. My sudden marriage. My bitter bride.

"Sasha," Igor pants. He's restless in the bed, thrashing his legs under the covers like he can't breathe. Or is in pain. His lips are turning blue. "Come."

When she doesn't move, I place a gentle hand at her lower back and propel her forward to his side. The nurse dribbles a dropper of medicine in his mouth. He reaches for his daughter's hand.

"Sasha," he says again.

"What is it?" I hear the tears in Sasha's voice. Anger, too.

"Trust...Maxim," he tells her.

Goosebumps race across my skin, up and down my arms and legs. On the back of my neck. Igor's fears for her life may be more substantial than I initially guessed. Or he's afraid Sasha will bolt.

Blyat.

He takes a short breath. Then nothing.

"Igor!" Galina cries.

"Papa?" Alarm rings out in Sasha's voice.

Igor breathes again.

"Oh!" Galina heaves a sigh.

But it was his last breath. His body twitches as the life goes out of it.

For the first time, Galina looks at me. "He waited to die until you got here," she says, but it's an accusation not a compliment.

I waited too long to come. I dodged his calls, not wanting to find out what it was he wanted to give me before he died.

I was afraid it would be his position as head of the Moscow bratva. Or some other high up position. I thought he was calling me back to service.

Never in a million years would I have guessed it was to wed his daughter.

"May the earth be soft for him," I murmur the traditional Russian saying then turn and walk out.

I don't have time to grieve the loss of a man who already threw me out of his life six years ago. I need to figure out how to keep his stubborn daughter safe when she has no desire to be attached to me.

asha

"WHERE ARE you going with that? Stop! That's my mom's," I snap at Viktor, one of my father's men. He's one of four jerks who just barged into the one-bedroom apartment I've lived in for the last year with boxes and started packing everything up today. Right now, he's boxing up the salad bowl I borrowed from my mom last week.

"I'm just following orders," he tells me.

Maxim's orders. Funny how Maxim doesn't even have a position in the organization, but these guys obey him.

Maxim also gave me orders via text this morning: *say your goodbyes and pack two suitcases because we're leaving this afternoon.*

Unlike Viktor and Alexei and the other two soldiers, I didn't obey.

I'm not going anywhere with Maxim. I don't know what kind of twisted game of poetic justice my father was playing with our lives, but marrying me to a man who hates me tops the cake.

My mom, whose apartment—the one I grew up in—is next door, comes in without knocking, taking in the chaos. "Today you leave," she says. A statement, not a question.

I shake my head. "No. Help me—they won't listen. Tell them to stop packing my stuff. I'm not going anywhere."

My mom grabs my hand and pulls me into my half-packed bedroom. When she finds there's a guy in there, too, she pulls me into the bathroom and shuts the door.

"Listen to me, Sasha," she whisper-snaps.

I shake off her hand. "What?"

"You *will* go. Your father left me nothing. *Nothing*. He left it all to Vladimir and to you, in care of your former lover."

"He wasn't my—"

My mom waves an impatient hand. "Whatever. Maxim controls it now. So you need to go with him, make nice and ensure that money stays where it's supposed to stay —*with us*."

I stare at her. I'm surprised to discover this side of her. She was always so passive, so compliant with my father. She took what he gave us and never asked for more.

But I suppose with him gone, she's discovering her vulnerability to losing it all. We both are.

The rebel in me wants to tell her *hell no*. I have principles, and they don't allow me to be sold off to another member of my father's organization.

But I have no livelihood and neither does she. My American acting degree is useless both here and there. The only job I worked was a side gig in college that involved me dressing sexy and handing out whatever product we were pushing. And I only did it for fun—not for the money.

Honestly? I shouldn't have to work. My father's money was intended for us, he just was an asshole about the way he gave it to us.

"What about Vladimir? He's supposed to provide for you." I hadn't brought myself to ask about him before because I knew I couldn't keep my mouth shut about how wrong this all is.

My mother clenches her teeth. "Vladimir is supposed to provide for me, yes. But you get everything. And I have no guarantees Vladimir will hold up his end of the bargain. *You will not give up our inheritance because you're being a stubborn cow.*"

I draw back, surprised at how mean and desperate she sounds. Like she's inches from a nervous breakdown. Or doing something crazy.

"I won't give it up," I promise her. "Maxim and I will come to an arrangement." That was my plan from the start. He doesn't want to be saddled with me any more than I want to be his devoted wifey. All we have to do is acknowledge that, and we can forego the whole moving in together and pretending. I'll stay here. He'll send me a check every month. Or better yet, direct deposit.

I head back out to the kitchen where Viktor's nearly packed up everything. He looks over, but his gaze goes past me to my mother. "You okay, Galina? Anything I can do for you?"

He's been our bodyguard for as long as I can remember. He and Alexei, the other guard, live here in the same building and rotate their time babysitting us. I suppose they're happy to be rid of me. But it suddenly occurs to me that Viktor may not feel the same about my mother. The way he looks at her...

How did I never notice that before?

"You can help my mom by leaving my shit alone," I tell

him. "Put that down!" I snap, when he tosses my expensive blender in a box.

"Take it easy." Maxim walks in my front door like he owns the place. Maybe he does—who knows?

He's impeccably dressed, as always, in a crisp blue button-down and tailored slacks. His hands are in his pockets in that GQ-casual way he has of standing. Like nothing ever ruffles him.

The past week has been a nightmarish blur with the funeral and interment. I've been numb, trying to help my mom bear her grief. Too angry to even examine my own. Maxim kept his distance, and I was hoping it meant he had as little interest in maintaining this sham marriage as I do.

But it appears I was wrong. And now I regret not trying to talk to him yesterday before he set all this into motion. To talk him out of this insanity.

"All your things get shipped to Chicago. If there's something you want to leave for your mom, just tell them, and they'll separate it out."

I fold my arms across my chest. "I'm not going to Chicago."

"It's not up for discussion," he says easily, almost like he expected that response but gives it no credence. His gaze dips to my breasts, which are pushed up and framed by my folded arms. I wore a skin-tight, pink-gold minidress today, which I've been using to fluster all the men swarming around my apartment this morning.

I'm way more satisfied than I should be to find Maxim is also affected by it.

"Listen." I switch into English since we both speak it, and my father's men don't. "I understand you control the money now. I'm fine with that. I'll be a good girl and do what you tell me. But we don't have to pretend to be husband

and wife. I know you don't want me, and I obviously don't want you."

"The marriage isn't about what we want, *caxapok*."

His old endearment for me—*sugar*—rolls off his tongue too glibly and sends a riot of the shame and longing he once incited blasting through me again as if I were still seventeen.

"Your father wanted you safe, and he chose me to be your protector."

I gesture toward the men dismantling my apartment. "Viktor and Alexei will keep me safe, as they always have."

Even though we're speaking English, Maxim takes a step closer and drops his voice. "Think about it, *caxapok*. If your father thought you were safe with them, he wouldn't have arranged to have you shipped off to America. He wouldn't have brought me in."

I want to scoff. My mom and I practically own Viktor and Alexei.

After I got Maxim banished, I realized how much power I could wield with my sexuality. And since it's the only power I wielded in my life, I used it. I played games with my father's men. Baiting them, getting on my knees for them. Sucking their cocks. Then threatening to tell my father to get whatever I needed from them—usually my freedom.

But a whisper of foreboding runs through me at Maxim's words. He's right. With my father dead, everything's changed. I don't hold any power anymore.

"Go and pack your personal things. Our flight is in a couple of hours."

I shake my head mulishly. "I'm not going."

Maxim goes still and warning bells go off in my head. There's a dangerous air to him. "Pack now or you travel with what I bring for you."

"Just leave me here," I try again. "You can have the

money—that's why I'd be in danger, right? So you keep it. Just give me enough to live on, and I'll stay out of your hair. Just leave me here."

"Do you think I married you for the fucking money?" he snarls. Maxim's upper lip curls. He shouldn't look so beautiful when he looks down his nose scornfully at me. "Believe me, *caxapok*, I don't want it. It—*and you*—are definitely more trouble than you're worth."

I spread my hands. "Then *go*. I'm letting you off the hook. Vladimir will protect me here."

"I made a promise to your father, Sasha. I won't dishonor him by forsaking it."

I roll my eyes.

He looks at his watch. "We're running out of time, sugar. Looks like you're traveling with what's already packed. Go and get in the car that's waiting outside."

I don't know why I have to push. Stubbornness has always been my downfall. I fold my arms across my chest, lift my chin and dare to say, "Fuck you."

He cocks his head. I half expect a slap, like my father sometimes issued, but he appears completely unruffled. "If I have to make you, there will be consequences, Sasha."

"Go ahead—make me," I challenge.

Maxim isn't amused. He loses the relaxed posture and launches into motion, like the sleeping lion that suddenly springs into a pounce. In one swift movement, he tosses me over his shoulder and carries me to the door, barking an order at one of the men to get my suitcases and bring them down to the car.

His hand claps down on my ass when we're out in the hall. "There are consequences for your disobedience, *caxapok*."

Surprisingly, he doesn't sound angry. His voice is relaxed

and even, despite the exertion of carrying me. I wriggle on his shoulder, which sends my microskirt bunching up around my waist. He slaps my ass again, kicking open the door to the stairs instead of waiting for the elevator. "Stop squirming, or we'll both break our necks," he advises as he starts swiftly down the steps.

I find the back of his belt and hang onto it. His muscular ass fills his slacks, flexing as he takes each stair. Heat swirls in my lower belly as my old attraction to this man flares to life. I remember what he looked like on the deck of my father's yacht. His shirt off, skin bronzed in the sun. He was an Adonis, sculpted muscle and perfect lines, in the prime of his youth.

He's no less appealing now, at thirty.

He exits the building, and I reach back to tug my hemline down, fuming that he's giving a show to his driver and the men outside. He tips me down to my feet, and when the driver opens the back door of the waiting car, hustles me inside the roomy Towncar.

Maxim says something to the driver before he climbs in beside me and shuts the door, then snaps the window between the front seat and back closed. The way he looks at me makes everything inside me squirm. There's a dark promise in his gaze. Like he's going to enjoy punishing me.

There will be consequences.

I try to control my blush—one of the downsides of being a redhead. "So what? You're going to punish me, as my father suggested?" I'm a fool to keep pushing. But it's Maxim, and I never recovered from him spurning me as a teen.

I swear I see the corners of his lips twitch right before he tugs me down across his knees.

I'm simultaneously thrilled and horrified. My body's

already a live wire from being ignominiously manhandled by him out of the building. Now, with the promise of punishment, electricity zings everywhere.

He gives me several hard spanks—five, to be exact—then he squeezes my ass roughly. My minidress rides up my hips, exposing the lower portion of my ass. I'm wearing a thong since the dress shows everything, so Maxim now has a full view of my cheeks.

I don't make a sound. I'm breathing hard, but it's more from shock than pain although a tingle and burn start to set in as he continues to knead and massage my ass.

It feels good. Humiliating, but hot. And when his fingers stroke between my legs, over the thong, I realize just how much Maxim is still my ideal man.

I fell in love—or maybe it was just lust—with him on that yacht in Croatia, and even though things went terribly wrong, it seems the attraction never died. Heat pulses between my legs. Maxim rubs along the seam of my panties, tracing the string up between my ass cheeks and back down again. I soak the little triangle of fabric, impossibly excited.

The moment he slides a finger under my panties, though, my internal alarms come back online. I buck on his lap.

The truth is, I've never let a man touch me there. I flaunted and bluffed my sexual experience to rebel against my father, but in the end, I actually was that good little girl he wanted me to be.

And Maxim may think he can do whatever he wants with me, that he has rights to my body because we stood in front of a clerk and he gave me my father's ring, but it's not going to happen.

I lurch my legs toward the floor of the car, and he lets me go. I land on my knees at his feet. "I'm not having sex with you," I declare, my mussed hair falling across my face.

Maxim gives me an unfathomable look. He was always hard to read. "I hope you're good at satisfying yourself, then, because no other man will be getting between those legs."

I flush with indignation—probably to a darker red than my hair, but before I can think of a response, Maxim's door opens, and one of the men hands in my purse. "I'll put the suitcases in the trunk," he tells Maxim then steals a glance at me kneeling at my husband's feet and smirks.

"Don't look at her," Maxim orders, slamming the door in the guy's face. He grips my elbow and helps me back onto the seat beside him. "I'm sorry for that," he surprises me by saying. "He should have knocked first."

"I guess you think you own me," I seethe, still hung up on the claim he's made on my body.

"I think you're my wife," Maxim says flatly, somehow conveying what a pain in the ass that is to him. "And I promise I'll kill any man who touches you."

CHAPTER 3

axim

THE BLUSH BLEEDS from Sasha's face at my threat. The car lurches into motion, en route to the airport. I shift to make room for the tightness in my pants.

I didn't mean to humiliate her with the spanking, but when she suggested punishment I just couldn't help myself. Her ass was so damn tempting in that body-hugging dress she's wearing, and she's been begging for a correction since I showed up today.

Judging by how wet she got, she enjoyed it as much as I did. But I shouldn't have tried to satisfy her. There's zero trust between us right now. Besides, if she hadn't pulled away, that jackal who opened the door would've gotten even more of an eyeful than he did.

"I suppose the same rules won't apply to you?"

"I won't be letting any men between my legs, no." I'm being a dick, I know, but she's already such a pain in my ass,

23

RENEE ROSE

I don't know how I'm going to stand this marriage. I learned at a young age that women are lying manipulators, and I know Sasha is one of the worst of them.

"You'll be screwing anyone you want while you keep me under lock and key. Is that how it works?"

I attempt to shove my irritation down. Try to muster some understanding and compassion. It's not her fault she thinks the worst of me. Her father modeled all the lowest male behaviors. I grip her hair and tug her head back, then slide my mouth down the column of her neck. "If you want a different arrangement, *caxapok*, then claim me." I open my mouth wide and bite her breast over the dress and her bra.

Her beautiful chest heaves like she's a damsel in a corset, swooning over the bold touch of her gentleman courter.

I kiss her clavicle, the hollow of her throat. Trail my tongue down between her breasts. She smells delicious—like citrus and spices. Like sunshine and summer. My dick gets harder than stone. Now that I've touched her—now that I've felt how soft and luscious her body is, how responsive—the leash on my control grows short.

"Are you telling me you'd be faithful if I had sex with you?" The wobble in her voice belies the bold tone.

"Yes," I shock myself by saying.

Huh. I never imagined I'd commit to one woman. Then again, I never imagined I'd marry. Especially not to a wealthy young wilful bride whose life I have to protect. But no, I wouldn't fuck around on her. Not if we had a real marriage.

She arches her full round tits up when I bite the fabric over her nipple. "I-I don't believe you." Her breath is short. Her hands find their way to my shoulders.

"Give it up, Sasha," I coax, "and I'll save myself for you."

24

She gives me a firm push, and I immediately release her and sit back in my seat. I may force her onto the airplane today, but I don't pressure women to have sex. That's not me. Ever.

"I'm not your whore," she says.

I narrow my eyes, the ache in my balls making me cranky. *Why the fuck would she even say that?* "No, you're my wife. And the sooner you accept that, the easier this will be for both of us."

"I have no intention of making this easy for you." She folds her arms and then her long, bare legs.

"Careful, Sasha," I warn. "That road goes both ways."

After a stretch of silence, she mutters sullenly, "I don't have my passport."

It was passed to me with all the paperwork related to our marriage, the trust, and Igor's will. Apparently, Igor had taken it from her and kept it in his safe. The passport and her birth certificate are in her mother's surname. Igor was careful not to mark her as a target with his. I'll give her mine, though. I don't have people gunning for me like Igor did. She's the one who will bring danger to me, so I need to signal to any potential enemies she's permanently under my wing. "I have it."

She rolls her eyes. "Of course you do. Because women can't be trusted to keep their own documentation."

Against my better judgment, I reach into my travel case pocket and pull out her passport. I don't trust her not to run, so it's probably a terrible idea to give it to her, but we're going to have to learn to trust each other at some point. I hand it to her. "I trust you, sugar," I lie.

She blinks in surprise then studies me suspiciously before putting it in her purse.

I pull out my wallet and take out a credit card and hand it

to her. "You can use this if you need it. Vladimir already closed the accounts on the cards your father gave you."

She frowns. "He did?" She shakes her head. "What an asshole."

I nod my agreement. "Do you trust him to take care of your mother?"

She goes still and gives me a sidelong look then slowly shakes her head. "No. I think my dad must've been losing his mind when he cooked up that arrangement. All of the arrangements."

"Meaning you don't trust me, either?"

She shrugs. "It feels like punishment. I was never the sweet, doting daughter he wanted me to be. Why else would he pin me to the one guy in his organization who has the biggest reason to hate me? He must be cackling from the grave right now."

I make a non-committal sound and look out the window. Do I hate her for what she did? For lying about me and getting me thrown out of Igor's cell?

Maybe I did when it happened. It solidified my feelings about women as lying, manipulative pains in the ass. I don't know if I still do. Yes, I think she's a petulant and spoiled *mafiya* princess, but I also know she is exactly what Igor made her.

Is it possible she's not in any danger, and this was just Igor's final punishment to us both? That he enacted some kind of rich irony to couple us together after we fucked each other over so well last time. That his money is not actually what's putting Sasha in danger, it's the glue that keeps us bound?

I suppose.

But I doubt it. I know the workings of the bratva. This is

one of Igor's many machinations, yes, but I still believe it was because he trusted me to keep Sasha alive.

He wasn't sure about the men he kept closest to him in Moscow.

"I don't hate you for the past," I say, finally, still looking out the window. "But I'm not above punishing you." Igor planted the seed that I would exact retribution with her. After experiencing how pleasurable it was to spank her gorgeous ass, I'm not inclined to let her off the hook.

I sense a shiver run through her. I steal a glance where she sits beside me. Her pouty lips are parted, and I see a flash of both excitement and vulnerability. A glimpse of that beautiful, underloved teenager, desperate for attention from any quarter and seeking it from me.

But the moment she realizes I'm looking, her mouth snaps closed, and she lifts her chin. "Maybe I'll be punishing you," she sniffs.

Fuck.

Me.

Maybe this all was Igor's big, sick joke.

Sasha

Maxim pays someone at the curb to take our bags and check us in, so we can go straight to the security line. There, he pays someone for us to cut in line.

I've forgotten how nice it is to travel with a powerful man. It's not that I didn't have money in my purse when I went back and forth between California and Moscow. But it wasn't the same. I've been sheltered my whole life. My years at USC were off the charts fun—having freedom and developing friendships —but I was still just a college student. I had no power.

I didn't know how to grease wheels or who to bribe. But maybe that's only a secret club for men, anyway. Women rely on their beauty to get special favors. It's always worked for me.

My minidress gets me plenty of attention. Honestly, it's way more something I'd wear to go out dancing at a night-club than something to travel in. Ditto on the platform sandals. I wore it to get under Maxim's skin, still under the impression I'd be able to talk him out of dragging me to Chicago.

But here I am in the airport showing way too much skin. Oh well, I might as well own it. I toss my hair and cock a hip, pretending I'm a movie star, and that's why we get to cut in line.

Maxim loops an arm around my waist and draws me closer to him. My breast brushes against his chest, my nipple puckering in my bra. My panties are still wet from his spanking in the car.

I arch a brow but don't pull away. I was expecting a rebuke or the crankiness my father used to show when he thought I looked slutty. I like Maxim's response quite a bit better. "Staking your claim?" I purr.

"Damn straight." He looks around. "It's either that or kill every man who looks at you, and I don't think that would go over in an airport." He gazes down, standing taller than me, even in the platform heels. "I seem to recall you have a streak of exhibitionism in you," he says.

I blink, startled by the observation.

"So I figure I'd better accept it, or I'll spend the rest of my life mopping blood from the floor."

I'm even more surprised by his chosen response. Do I have a streak of exhibitionsim in me? My mother always said I was a show-off. My father told me to stop begging for attention.

But Maxim doesn't say it like it's a character flaw. He makes it sound like a kink. Something sexy and hot, not cloying and weak.

I fight to swallow, suddenly remembering why it was I fancied myself in love with Maxim when we were in Croatia. Because he actually *sees* me. He pays attention. He may be the only man in my life who looked past the red hair and pretty face. Even when I didn't know who I was, he seemed to. I remember sitting on the deck, watching the dolphins play in the water as we played cards and listened to music together. While my father was smoking cigars with his men or screwing my mother in their cabin, Maxim was the only one who noticed my existence.

That was why I offered myself up on a platter for him.

Like an idiot.

"As long as everyone knows you're with me, we have no problems, sugar." He pulls me closer, angling my body into his, so his thigh comes between mine like we're doing a sexy lambada on the dance floor. "You have it, you might as well flaunt it." He gives me a wink, and I melt even more.

Damn him.

I squeeze my inner thighs together around his thicker limb. It would serve him right if I left a wet spot on his pant leg.

He doesn't seem to mind a bit. His hand strays lower, rounding over my ass. "They can look all they want," he murmurs. "And you can give them a show. Just as long as they don't try to touch."

The security officer calls us forward and checks our

tickets and passport. Maxim keeps me tucked at his side. My skin tingles with the nearness of him, but more than that, a strange satisfaction filters through me. Knowing Maxim's proud I'm with him is a new sensation. Granted, it's just because I'm pretty arm candy—exactly what my mother was to my father—but I still like the feeling. There's an intoxicating power to it. One I guess I've been seeking my whole life but rejected every chance of having because I refused to ever give myself to a man. I played the cock-tease, baiting the hook and then casting them back in the ocean.

Now, I have no choice. I belong to Maxim. And in this instance, he doesn't seem sorry about that fact.

That doesn't mean I'm going to lie back and spread my legs for him. It doesn't mean I'm going to play nice or be sweet or any of the things my medieval father expected of me. But things could be worse.

My husband thinks I'm hot and will let me flaunt it.

Fabulous. Because that is the one thing I've always enjoyed and been good at.

CHAPTER 4

axim

"I'M NOT HAVING sex with you," Sasha declares again in Chicago after I lead her by the elbow, past my boss and his pregnant lover and the rest of my suite-mates into my bedroom.

She's unimpressed by the grandeur of the Kremlin—the name the neighborhood gave to Ravil's twenty-story building with a view of Lake Michigan. I don't bring women home to my suite a lot, but they usually drool over the penthouse I share with the upper echelon of the brotherhood—the more than half a story made into our private bratva mansion.

"Worried you can't satisfy me?" I toss at her.

For an instant, I see her confidence slip, like I poked a wound. Right—probably the one I left when I rejected her back on that yacht in Croatia. In a flash, though, she covers it with a sniff and a toss of her long red mane. "As if," she throws back, going to stand by the wall of windows to look out at the lights of the boats out on the water. She's been speaking English since we got on the plane, and apart from the light accent, she sounds exactly like an American college student.

Despite it all, despite what she did to me, I still feel protective of her. Maybe because I saw the way her father treated her. Saw the beautiful, hurt teenager desperate to be loved.

She may be an adult now, but I still see through her bravado.

I set her suitcase on my dresser and walk over. "I didn't mean that, *caxapok*." I lightly touch her upper arms, insinuating my body against her backside without quite making contact. Close enough, so I can feel her little intake of breath. See the goosebumps that raise on her neck. Relish the subtle heat from her body. "It's my job to satisfy you." I lower my head and brush my lips over her shoulder. "And believe me, doll, you would be satisfied."

She stops breathing.

It's not that I'm dying to consummate this marriage. Although Sasha is hot as fuck, and the chemistry between us is still explosive. I'm just thinking sex might take the edge off. Give us a place to start.

She hates that her father traded her like he was selling a thoroughbred horse. She hates that he picked me, the man who humiliated her right when she was coming into her own sexuality. She especially hates that I control her purse-strings now.

I'm not so thrilled with being saddled with her, myself. But Igor won my loyalty when he saved my life and took me under his wing as a young man, and that loyalty didn't die when he banished me.

I'd love to park Sasha in some apartment and pretend she

doesn't exist, but I can't. Her life's in danger, and I'm responsible for keeping her safe. So like it or not, we'll be in each other's faces. Likely for the rest of our lives.

So we might as well make the best of it.

"Not happening." Sasha's shut-down is weakened by the wobble in her voice, the breathless quality of her words.

My dick punches out against my zipper. I slip my hands under her arms to coast down her sides. Her body melts back against mine. I splay one hand over her belly, bring the other to squeeze her breast. "You're mine now, Sasha," I murmur against her ear. "You might as well enjoy the benefits."

Her knees wobble. I flick my tongue against her ear, draw her earlobe between my lips and suck. I find her nipple beneath the padding of her bra and pinch it.

She grips my hands and tugs them away, spinning to face me. "Not happening." Her pupils are blown, cheeks flushed. "I want a separate bedroom."

I shake my head. "Not happening."

A seconds-long staredown happens. I can see her gears churning, and I doubt I'm going to like whatever they produce.

"I'm never having sex with you," she asserts.

"Oh, I think you will. But it won't be because I force you, sugar. No, you'll be begging me for it. And I promise you'll enjoy it."

For some reason, that promise seems to make her confidence slip for a flash, but she lifts her chin. "Dream on, my friend." She tosses her hair and heads to the en suite bathroom. I hear the bathtub start, so I undress and crawl in bed. I didn't let myself sleep on the sixteen-hour flight, knowing we'd arrive in Chicago at night, so I'm fucking exhausted. I watched the movies they showed on the flight, but Sasha watched her own entertainment on her iPad—

episode after episode of *Downton Abbey*. I don't know why it surprised me, but it did. When I asked, she said she loved historicals.

I guess I thought she'd be watching something insipid. Some stupid romcom thing. But I have to remember she studied theatre. It makes sense she has a thing for period pieces.

I leave the bedside lamp on and doze off, waking when she emerges.

Naked.

I mean, completely naked—no towel wrapped around her, just her pale skin and—*aw fuck*—the most beautiful pair of tits I've ever seen. I get fully hard before my gaze has even traveled lower, past the soft mound of her belly to glimpse her—*Gospodi*—bare sex.

Either she shaved for me in there, or she's been recently waxed.

Fuck. Me.

"What are you doing?" I ask as she walks over to the bed and pulls the covers down to climb in.

"I sleep naked," she says.

First of all—bullshit. *Yerunda*. Second, she's not going to play this sex manipulation game with me. Not again. It ends now.

"Sugar, you climb in this bed naked, I will fuck you so hard and so well you won't walk right tomorrow."

She freezes. Her nipples tighten like bolts, and I see goosebumps race across her skin. She straightens and cocks a hip, one hand on her waist. "You said you wouldn't force me."

I shrug. "If you want me to hold back, *caxapok*, you keep your clothes on. That's all I'm going to say."

We lock gazes. Her perfect breasts lift and lower with her

rapid breathing. Whatever she sees in my face must tell her I'm not fucking around because she turns away. "Fine."

I watch the twitch of her gorgeous ass as she struts to the dresser. I think she's going to open her suitcase, but instead, she opens and shuts my drawers until she finds one with my t-shirts. She pulls on a soft cotton undershirt and comes to bed. No panties. Just my fucking white shirt. She crawls in with her back to me.

All I can think about is that bare fucking pussy within reaching distance. How much I want to push open her knees and lick her until she screams. Give her everything she wanted from me all those years ago.

I flick off the lamp. "You're playing a dangerous game, Sasha."

"It's the only one I know," she says into the darkness.

Her words pierce through my irritation at her cock-tease, the haze of testosterone, to land somewhere in my chest with a sharp jab. The honesty of her answer cuts me off at the knees. Of course, it's the only one she knows.

Sex is the only weapon she's been taught to wield.

This is why I need to work harder to disarm her. I roll on my side and loop an arm around her waist, dragging her backward until her ass meets my lap. With great effort, I will my erection down as she stiffens and stops breathing.

I kiss her shoulder. "You're mine now," I tell her softly. "Which means we're on the same team. Stop fighting me."

She continues to hold her breath. I feel her belly flex against my arm, and then she lets out her breath on a sob.

I pull her tighter. Aw, fuck. She just lost her father, with whom she had a complicated relationship with at best. She got married off like a medieval bride to a guy she doesn't trust not to break her.

She sucks in her breath and holds it again.

"Let it out," I murmur against her nape. "You've had a hell of a week."

She doesn't breathe, though. She keeps holding it until my own lungs feel like they'll burst out of sympathy, and then she wallops me in the eye with her elbow.

"*Blyat*." I release her, but she turns in the darkness and strikes out at me again.

My reflexes fire too quickly, and I catch her wrists, holding her captive before I realize she needs this tantrum. I let her go, and she attacks me, sobbing as she pummels me with her fists. She must not want to hurt me, though, because she picks up a pillow and uses it, instead, to whack me over the head and shoulders.

I let the blows fall, listen to her sobbing breath and whimpers until they slow, then I take the pillow from her. "Enough." I pin her wrists down beside her head, my body blanketing hers.

She whimpers again, an angry sob. My mouth crashes down on hers. She tastes of tears and toothpaste. I slide my lips over her softer ones, dragging her lower lip into my mouth, then going at it again, flicking my tongue between her lips.

She kisses me back, moaning softly into my mouth.

I catch myself grinding in the notch between her legs, and I stop myself. This isn't about sex. I'm not going to force that issue. I just want to give her the connection she craves. Bind the two of us together with something besides bitter words and an ugly past.

Our lips twist and tangle. I slow the claiming.

"Enough," I murmur again, possibly more to myself than her, and force myself off of her. I slide once more to her side, rolling her to face away from me and looping an arm around her waist. "Go to sleep, *caxapok*. We can fight more in the morning."

Her breath rasps quick and frantic for a few more minutes then slows to normal and eventually into slumber.

Only then do I let myself drift into a much-needed sleep.

CHAPTER 5

$\mathcal{S}$*asha*

M AXIM GETS UP FIRST, waking me as he climbs out of bed. I pretend to be asleep. I don't know why—I guess because I'm not ready to face him.

Not after last night.

The way I broke down in front of him. The way he kissed me. At least it was dark. I didn't have to look into his handsome face after he's seen so much of me.

The real me, I mean. Not just the naked me.

I hear the shower turn on, and the urge to run comes over me.

It's a literal urge—I'm a morning jogger—but also an emotional one.

I'm not running away from Maxim permanently. That would accomplish nothing. He controls my cash. And my mother's. I wish I could say I'm one of those girls who gives the middle finger to money and walks away, but I'm not ready for that. And my mom needs me to do this.

Maxim claims my father put him in charge to keep me safe. Well, I don't mind letting him scramble a bit to make that happen, then.

Same thing I used to do to the guards my father assigned to protect us.

I get up and quietly put on a pair of yoga pants, a jogging bra, and sneakers. I pull my hair up into a high ponytail and smile to myself. Me going out in nothing but a jogging bra might give him a conniption alone.

No, that's wrong. He told me yesterday I should flaunt it. That unfamiliar sense of warmth snakes through me again.

I quickly and silently pull on my sneakers and shoes and slip out the bedroom door.

There are guys in the living room, the same as last night.

Maxim hadn't bothered to introduce me to everyone, but some I recognized. Ravil, obviously, their *pakhan*.

I didn't get to meet his mistress, the pretty blonde who'd been curled up with him on the couch. She looked pregnant, which goes against bratva rules. Of course, my father had a child, too, but he kept us secreted away. We never lived with him. He never married my mother or officially claimed me as his daughter until he put me in his trust.

There's no sign of Ravil and his pretty girlfriend this morning, but a young man in a Matrix t-shirt sits at a table in the living room, working at a computer. Another, who looks just like him—must be his twin—stands in the kitchen. The beefy guy who stands well over six and a half feet high and is almost as broad leans on the breakfast bar, eating scrambled eggs from a frying pan.

"Good morning," I say brightly in English. It's nice to

practice my English again, and I noticed they all spoke it with each other last night.

"The princess emerges," the twin in the kitchen says.

I flip him off.

He chuckles. "I'm Nikolai. We weren't properly introduced last night."

I pass him without offering my hand. "I'm going for a run," I chirp.

"Maxim!" the other twin calls out. "Your bride is running away." His tone of voice is more like the one you'd use when asking your roommate to bring a glass of water than a real alarm, and I find myself liking these guys, despite myself. They bear the same bratva tattoos but seem casual and friendly. Nothing like my father's men back home.

At the same time, the giant guy moves faster than I could've predicted, getting up from the breakfast bar and blocking the doorway.

I expected as much. I've lived with overbearing security guards my whole life. I definitely know how to deal with them. I press my body up against the giant's. "You must be the bodyguard," I purr, trailing a finger across his meaty forearm, which is folded over his chest.

"Sasha," Maxim growls a warning from the doorway to our bedroom suite. I hear his wet feet slap against the floor as he comes toward me.

I don't look his way, but I answer him. "Oh, you don't like it when I touch him, do you?" I purr and stroke up the enforcer's biceps.

The giant snatches up my wrist to stop me at the same moment Maxim snaps, "*Don't touch her.*"

Exactly as expected. As I said, I've been playing this game my whole life. Still, the jolt of pleasure at hearing

Maxim claim me is infinitely more satisfying than when it was my father or one of his henchmen.

The giant immediately releases his hold on me as if scalded. Maxim's men are as loyal as my father's. I wasn't sure, since he isn't *pakhan* here. Good to know.

But then Maxim does something my father would never do.

"Please," he tempers his previous sharp command to the brute, his voice more controlled now. He arrives by my side. "Thank you." There's an apology in his voice.

Not for me, though. He takes hold of my ponytail and uses it to tug my head backward. He's in nothing but a peach towel wrapped around his waist. Water droplets still drip down his muscled and tattooed chest.

The giant slips away, leaving me with my wet and annoyed husband.

"I told you, *caxapok*. They can look, but not touch." His growl is almost a purr, too, like he enjoys manhandling me. His brown eyes burn intensely, but he doesn't seem angry. There's a bruise on the eyebrow of his right eye, and I realize, with a shock, that I probably gave it to him.

I try not to show any intimidation. This part I'm not used to. My father used to slap and berate me, but dominance in the way Maxim wields it—sexual dominance—is something altogether different, and my body reacts accordingly. Embers spark and flame in my lower belly.

I stretch my lips into a smile. "You didn't say I couldn't touch them."

"New rule, then." His eyes leave my face, dipping to my breasts, which are pushed up and pinned together by the jogging bra. His gaze returns, darker than before. "Don't fuck with me on this, Sasha or things will get very messy." He bites my earlobe. "But you like messy, don't you?" He releases my ponytail but cages my throat with his tattooed fingers. He squeezes just enough for me to register his control but not enough to block my airflow. Then he lowers his lips to mine.

My feminine parts clench and flutter with excitement at his supple lips caressing mine. And it is a caress—totally at odds with his chokehold on me. It's not a brutal, controlling kiss, not that I would've minded that, either.

When he pulls away, he rubs his lips together like he's relishing the taste of my mouth. His hand still holds me captive.

I blink up at him, more disoriented by the kiss than all the rest of it. "D-did I give you that bruise?"

He takes a moment, just studying me, before he gives a barely perceptible nod.

"I'm sorry."

The corners of his lips quirk. Now he comes in for the hard kiss. The claiming one that I'd been expecting.

Flames lick between my legs as he plunders my mouth, his tongue sweeping between my lips, his lips devouring mine.

My panties are wet. Probably smoking.

I don't know what it's like to have sex, but I suddenly want it. Badly. Not with my fingers on my clit—with a man. This man.

The kiss goes on for long, breathless seconds. Long enough that I lose all orientation. The penthouse spins. I forget my agenda.

When Maxim pulls away, he releases my throat and gives me another sweeping gaze. "You wanted to go running?"

My head wobbles as I nod.

"I'll go with you. You don't leave here alone—I told you that last night."

Well, not exactly. He'd told the others I wasn't to leave alone, not me, specifically. But I've lost the will to argue, still trying to calm my hammering pulse and cool my lady parts.

Maxim takes my elbow and leads me to the barstool beside the giant. "Sit with Oleg. I'll be ready in a minute."

It's an order, but I don't resist, needing a moment to recombobulate. Needing to cross my legs and pinch them together to alleviate the throb of my clit.

I look at the man beside me, who is focused on his eggs. "So you're Oleg? The enforcer, I guess?"

The giant man doesn't look my way.

"He doesn't speak," Nikolai offers. He's now on the couch, flipping through channels.

I look him over, dropping some of my bad girl act. He's not deaf because he obviously heard Maxim's order not to touch me. I wonder whether his muteness is a choice or a physical limitation. He bears the tattoos proving he spent time in a Siberian prison. I wonder if something happened to him there.

The brother wearing the worn and faded Matrix t-shirt comes into the kitchen and opens the refrigerator. He opens a pizza box on the counter and pulls a slice out. "I'm sorry about your father," he says in English with his mouth full.

I shrug. "He's dead." It's about all I can find to say about him.

The young man flicks his brows. "Let me guess—Igor was a shitty father?"

I snort in surprise at the acknowledgement, the flicker of a smile tugging my lips. None of my father's men in Russia would have ever uttered such words. But we are out of his territory now.

"We were part of his cell before he kicked us to Ravil. I'm Dima, Nikolai's brother."

I find myself instantly liking the guy—and his brother by proxy. Probably for the sole reason that he called Igor a shitty father. Also, they have that instant familiarity thing that puts me at ease. And they don't stare at my boobs.

Maxim emerges in a pair of gym shorts and a t-shirt, running shoes on his feet. He looks at home in the clothes, like he runs on a regular basis. This development foils my plan of taking off running and making someone keep up and sends a nervous twitter through me. Maybe I'll be the one working hard to keep up with him.

"Let's go, sugar." He catches my elbow in that dominating way he has and steers me toward the door.

"Bye, guys!" I call out with false cheerfulness.

"Why do you do that?" Maxim asks when we get in the elevator.

I back as far away from him as I can, leaning against the opposite wall and pulling my foot up to my ass to stretch my quad. "What?"

"Act like you're too good for them. Or you're making fun of them."

Something dives in my belly and settles heavily as a stone. I've been called a bitch before—behind my back, mostly. So many times.

No one's ever asked me *why* I play the part, though. Almost like he knows it's an act—not my true personality.

Maxim's suddenly getting real with me.

I switch legs and shrug. "Am I supposed to pretend they're my friends? I didn't willingly move in with them. They got foisted on me, same as you did. Same as every bodyguard or babysitter my dad's saddled me with."

A muscle jumps in Maxim's jaw. "All right, let's get something straight," he snaps as the elevator door opens.

I charge out of it, but he catches my elbow again and swings me back.

"Don't run off on me." He glares down at me, a line between his brows. "Those men aren't your bodyguards. They're not your servants—they're not your babysitters. They weren't sent to spy on you. They are my fucking brothers."

The stone in my gut grows heavier.

"Yes, you did get saddled with me, sugar. And I got saddled with you. And we're going to make the best of it."

"Says you," I shoot back, but a terrible feeling of shame seeps in, fueled by that rock still sitting square in the middle of my stomach. I *was* acting like a bitch. I'm acting like the spoiled *mafiya* princess I've always been. The part I detest but play with aplomb.

But if I don't war with Maxim, I don't know what to do. I don't know how to be. And the sense of vulnerability that brings up nearly kills me.

Maxim doesn't release my elbow. He stares down at me with a troubled expression like he's trying to make a decision, but after several precariously long seconds, all he says is, "Come on, there's a path on the lakeshore that's nice to run."

A sense of relief floods me like he just let me off some hook I didn't know I was even on. He tips his head toward the glass doors of the elegant building.

He waves at the doorman, who is clearly bratva based on his tattoos.

We jog, side by side, on a paved path along the lake. I'm not used to the heat, and I'm soon dripping with sweat, but it feels good to move after the long flight yesterday and the slight jetlag I still feel.

We run in silence for half an hour or so. Maxim lets me

set the pace but keeps up easily. I was right—he's definitely a regular runner. "How long do you usually run?" he asks.

The truth is, I'm getting hot and tired, but now my pride is keeping me from saying anything.

I shrug. "I can keep going."

"Come here." He veers off the path and onto a city street, crossing an intersection, and slowing to a walk.

"What are we doing?"

He pushes through a convenience store door. "Buying some water. You look hot."

"It doesn't take much for a redhead to look hot," I mutter, but I'm secretly grateful he's looking out for me.

He buys a large bottle of electrolyte water, opens the cap and hands it to me.

I drink, thirstily, and hand it back, half empty.

He finishes a quarter of it and crushes the middle of it before he puts the cap back on. "So we could either go back the way we came, along the lake drive, or we could take it slower through the city blocks where it's a little shadier, but less of a breeze."

It's bizarre, but for the first time in my life, I feel like a grown-up. When I lived in L.A., I had the time of my life, partying with my college friends. But that was still me acting like a rebel. This feels different. One of my father's men is treating me like an equal. Asking what I want to do and waiting for my answer. I don't have to run and make him chase. I don't have to trick him—or manipulate him.

He's just standing there, waiting for me to make the call.

I reward him with a smile—not the *I have you by the balls* smile—a genuine one. "Lake path, for sure. But let me see that water bottle."

He hands it back to me, and I uncap it and dribble a

healthy amount down my cleavage, soaking my running bra. It isn't to fuck with him, it's because I'm hot.

All right, and maybe to fuck with him a little bit. As he pointed out, I do have a streak of exhibitionism in me.

For a moment, I think he's pissed, and maybe he is because he grips my ponytail and pulls it back to bare my throat. Then he licks a long line down my throat and across my collarbone to dip between my breasts.

My pussy's squeezing, and I'm breathless by the time he lifts his head. "You spilled some water," he says, as if in explanation.

My legs quiver—probably just from the run, but I'm suddenly acutely aware of it.

His gaze dips to my breasts, and my nipples tingle and burn in response.

I suddenly want him. Desperately.

All this pretending I don't, all this resistance seems stupid. I have a hot husband. Not just any hot husband, but the man who literally molded my view of what makes a man hot. When I look at all other guys, I'm measuring them in comparison to this one.

And he wants me now.

But that reminds me how he didn't want me once. Of my utter humiliation—how much that rejection burned. Nope. Not giving in. Let him suffer with blue balls. My virginity is the only thing I still have control of in my life.

I take off running the way we came and sense him quickly catch up. He slaps my ass when he does, in a hard, satisfying way, and then paces with me at my side. My butt tingles and burns as I run, igniting the memory of that spanking he gave me in the back seat of the car in Moscow. The way he touched me afterward.

Ack! I can't think about it. No sex.

I'm not having sex with Maxim.

But as I run, the friction between my legs persists, stoking the heat rather than alleviating it. I glance down and see my nipples protruding visibly under my wet jog-bra. Lord have mercy. I'd better run straight for the cold shower.

CHAPTER 6

 *axim*

I T TAKES all my willpower not to follow Sasha into the shower, shove her up against the tile and lick every inch of her body until she begs me to fuck her. My balls ache to get between those pale thighs, and I know she's getting as needy as I am, but I'm not the type to come on strong. This is obviously a long game.

A whole fucking lifetime.

Blyat, I still can't believe I have a wife.

I distract myself from my blue balls by finding her phone. I bring it to the living room and toss it to Dima, Russia's—and now America's—most formidable hacker. "Get her switched onto my account, will you?"

Dima catches the phone but shoots me a skeptical expression. "Do I look like your local Verizon rep?"

"You know what I need." I make a circle with my finger in the air.

"Uh huh." He still sounds skeptical, but he pops open the back of her phone and starts taking it apart, adding in the tracking chip which will work regardless of whether her phone is on.

"I need you to start tracking everyone who comes into the country from Russia."

Nikolai speaks up. "Every single person? For what?"

"Well, can you cross-reference them against every known member of Russian bratva?" I ask, looking toward Dima, who is shaking his head in a long-suffering manner.

"You want to know if someone's coming after her?" Nikolai asks.

"Yes."

"Couldn't anyone just hire a hit here?" Pavel pipes in.

"They won't be as connected here. It would be harder."

"I can set up some data analysis and name matching on all passengers from Russia," Dima admits. "It will be a pain in my ass, but it isn't hard. It will take me a couple of days, but I can have it search retroactively. But what if they get a new identity before they come?"

"Who is it you think will come and why?" Nikolai asks.

"If she dies, the trust goes to benefit her mother but controlled by Vladimir as trustee. He got saddled with Galina."

"So you think Vladimir will send someone."

"Yes."

"So we hack the hell out of their cell and hopefully hear of any plan before it's executed," Nikolai says.

I shrug. "If you can." It's hard to cheat a thief. I doubt we'll have much success hacking their cell, but then again, Dima is the best, and Nikolai is no slouch, either.

"For the phone, do you want the full stalker package? The Lucy?" Dima asks, referring to the complete access he gave himself to all the data input and output from Ravil's pregnant girlfriend's phone and laptop after Ravil kidnapped her.

"What's *the Lucy*?" Lucy picks that unfortunate moment to enter the living room. She has a constant glow—both from the pregnancy, and, I have to assume by the amount of time they spend locked in the bedroom together, the number of orgasms Ravil wrings from her.

Dima and Nikolai both clear their throats and look away in classic twin mirroring.

Pavel, our brigadier, says loudly, "Is that my phone ringing?" and gets up from the sofa and leaves.

"Nobody is tracking your data anymore," Ravil says smoothly, coming up behind her and spreading his hands over her swollen belly. The two of them arrived on the same page while I was away in Moscow, but things were rocky there for a while. I was afraid Ravil put our entire organization at risk over his unborn child by bringing Lucy here as his prisoner. And he's usually the most level-headed of all of us.

He kisses her neck. "I promise." He sends Dima a warning glance. "Tell her."

Dima holds his hands up in surrender. "I just do what I'm told." His appeal is to Lucy, alone.

She twists to look over her shoulder at Ravil. "And you told him—?"

"I'm telling him now. Stop tracking her data. Except for the locator." He nibbles her ear lobe. "I need to know where you are, *kotyonok*. For safety."

"And safety, of course, is the only reason I'm tracking my bride's location at all times," I plead as if Lucy is our judge. In a way, I suppose she is. As an outsider of the organization, an American, and a female attorney, she brings an entirely new perspective and sensibility to the penthouse.

She narrows her eyes at me. "You don't intend to keep her

locked up here, do you?"

"Not at all. I intend to help her make a life in Chicago. And not be killed by those who want her father's fortune. She's an actress. Do you have any theater connections?"

I spent most of the plane ride trying to figure out how to make things work with Sasha, and the one thing I came up with to keep her happy was to get her involved with theater. Give her some creative outlet to help her get over the burn of her father's unshared plan for her.

"No, but I can ask around." Lucy walks into the kitchen and rummages through the refrigerator for the perogies Ravil keeps on hand at all times for her.

"Where's my phone?" I turn to see Sasha standing in the doorway to our bedroom, wearing a pair of jean shorts and—

"Fuck no," I growl, launching myself toward her.

Fear and excitement flare in her eyes as I storm closer to my bride, who's wearing nothing but a goddamn black lace bra on top, her tits spilling out like a joyful celebration of youth and sex.

I toss her over my shoulder and carry her back into the bedroom, kicking the door shut with my heel.

"Fuck no," I repeat.

"What?" she asks, breathless, as I drop her onto her butt on the bed. "You said they could look."

"I changed my fucking mind," I growl. I scrub a hand over my face, pacing at the foot of the bed. She's dewy and flushed and beautiful. Like a woman about to be ravished.

By me.

She opens those bee-stung lips to say something, but it dies on her breath when I grasp her ankles and yank her legs down until they form a wide V around my waist. I switch my grip to her wrists, pinning them down beside her head as I grind my erection in the notch between her legs.

"That policy is predicated on me not having blue fucking balls," I snarl.

Her eyes widen, and she goes very still like she knows I'm a goddamn feral animal about to strike. About to claim my prey in a brutal manner.

I thrust against her, making her draw in a sharp breath. "And on me being at your side."

"Got it," she whispers, breathless.

"Yeah?" I'm still pissed—unquenched lust making my brain short-circuit.

"Yes." She licks her pouty lips. "Sorry."

I relax, half-sorry, myself, that I cowed her enough to apologize. I don't like seeing her diminished. I don't mind the push-pull between us—I like her fire. I don't even mind her games—to a certain extent.

I brush my lips across hers, then bite the lower one and drag it between my teeth until it emerges with a pop.

"This problem between us could be easily solved," I tell her. When her eyes search mine, I nudge between her legs again with my hardened cock.

Her legs tighten around my waist as she inhales. "*Nyet.*" She turns her face away, and I instantly pull back.

I honor a woman's *no.*

"Your loss, *caxapok.*" I offer my hand to help her off the bed. "Just be careful. At some point, my leash will snap."

When she takes my hand, I sense a tremble in her fingers. The blush on her cheeks enthralls me, but I act the part of the gentleman, pulling her to her feet and leaving her to get dressed as I hit the shower to rub one out for the second time this morning.

"You're killing me, *printsessa,*" I call out from the bathroom as I step under the spray.

"That's my plan," she sing-songs back.

asha

NEVER LEAVE an attention-hungry mafia princess home unattended.

I smile to myself as I whip out Maxim's credit card at O'hare airport and board the first plane to L.A.

Since my phone hasn't started ringing, I'll bet Maxim hasn't even figured out I'm gone yet.

Guess who's back in the States, bitches? I group text Ashley, Kayla, and Sheri, my three former housemates and besties from college. *I'm on my way to your place. Party tonight?*

OMG!!! Sheri is the first to respond. *Hell to the yes! Where are you now?*

About to board a plane for L.A. I text back.

From RUSSIA??!

No, Chicago. Be there in a couple of hours.

Kayla is the next to reply with a string of alcohol emojis and, *EEEEEEK! I get off at six. Can't wait to see you!*

Then Ashley: *Why didn't you tell us you were coming? I am so down with partying tonight. Can't wait!!!!! I'm home now.* Her text is followed by five lines of happy faces, cocktail drinks and party hat emojis.

There are several more additions and confirmations and party girl .gifs. I sit back and smile. My four years at USC were the best time in my life, and the place I made lasting friendships with women as nutty as I am. Getting to see them again is one good thing about my new situation. And honestly? I'm thrilled to be back in the U.S.—Moscow suffocated me.

I have no doubt Maxim will catch up to me before the night is through. Even if he didn't put a tracer in my phone, which I'm certain he has, I just used his credit card to buy my ticket.

But that's the point. To be a pain in his ass and make him chase. It's what I used to do to the bodyguards and spies my dad sent to watch over me. I intend to drive the man crazy. After all, he should earn the millions he just took control of, shouldn't he?

Still, I nibble my lower lip, hoping I haven't bitten off more than I can chew. Maxim has a way of getting under my guard that throws me off-balance. Which, if I'm truly honest, is the real reason I'm running off.

It was getting too intense back there.

For both of us.

After the coming out in my bra incident yesterday, Maxim made himself scarce, leaving me with nothing to do but watch television with his housemates.

He didn't come back until dinner time when he took me out to a nearby cafe for dinner, and he disappeared again when we got back. Well, that's not exactly true. I couldn't keep my eyes open because the time change caught up to me, and I went to bed early, leaving him in the living room.

This morning, he jogged with me but then was working with the twins at the computer all day. This afternoon he disappeared again.

I like to think his avoidance is because of his blue-ball situation. Something I'm not the slightest bit sorry for. But I didn't like the way it felt. To be ignored. Dumped. Locked in.

So the first time the living room emptied of people—what seems to be a rare occurrence there—I bailed. I grabbed my purse—the giant one I pre-packed with a few things and shut my bedroom door like I was locked inside reading. They may not notice I'm gone until Maxim returns.

The front door guy tried to stop me, but I got up in his face and pulled the bratva brat act. "Do you know who I am? No? I am Alexandra Antonova, daughter of Igor Antonov, Ravil's boss and wife of Maxim Popov. I can tell you my husband would not approve of you touching me or detaining me, right now."

The guy dropped his touch on my arm like I was made of fire. "One moment, Mrs. Popov. He told me not to let you go out unattended." The guy looked around, desperate for someone else to help him out—I'm sure he was debating whether it was worse to leave his post or to let me go.

I switched tactics and turned on the charm. "It's okay. Maxim knows I'm just running to the store to grab some *feminine hygiene* products." I whisper the feminine hygiene part.

He pulled back even more. "I'll tell Maxim what a great job you're doing manning your station down here. Thanks so much!" I waved my fingers individually and scooted out the door.

Dodging my security is a talent I've perfected.

Now I have my phone off, so Maxim can't reach me, and I'll be in L.A. by nightfall. Ready to tear up the town like old times.

Although with Maxim, there will certainly be consequences. I think of the way he tossed me over his lap and spanked my ass back in Russia and my lady parts warm. I'm totally warped because I'm actually hoping he does it again.

It excited me far more than I care to examine. But *he* excites me far more than I care to examine.

I pop my earbuds in my ears to watch reruns of *Game of Thrones*. After my *Downton Abbey* binge on the way over here, I'm still in the mood for period pieces. *Game of Thrones* seems fitting for my life now. That's what we're all playing with each other, after all.

Maxim

I RETURN to the penthouse with an emerald ring in my pocket with enough bling to be seen from the moon. It has tiny diamonds all around it and down the band, and I engraved it with our names. I hated seeing Igor's ring on Sasha's finger, the constant reminder of what a sham of a wedding we had. I hated the symbolism of it, too. Like she was really married to her father not me.

I open the door to the penthouse with a spring in my step, thinking I've finally done something right when it comes to her.

She's not in the living room. Nikolai and Dima are there,

arguing heatedly over the best way to segment and match data from the airlines.

"Where's Sasha, in my room?"

Dima spares me a glance. "*Da.* She's been in there for a while now."

A niggling of foreboding comes over me. Maybe I shouldn't have left her alone. I stride across the living room and throw open my door.

No Sasha.

And her big carry-on purse is gone.

Fuck.

Me.

I check in the bathroom even though I know she won't be there.

Gospodi. Women can never be trusted—they are always full of lies, deceit and tricks.

Unbidden, the memory of my mother's cruel deception replays like the horror movie I can never unsee.

I KNOW SHE'S LYING, but I don't want to believe it. I prefer to pretend everything is as she says.

"This is just a temporary thing, Max. I'll be back in a week or two—a month at the longest. Be good and do as you're told."

The director of the orphanage puts an arm around my shoulders, gently tugging me away from her.

Panic wells. I grasp my mother's arm and try to hold on as she pulls away from me.

The tears in her eyes glitter as proof she's lying.

She's not coming back.

I don't cry because she told me not to. I am a good boy. I do as I'm told. I eat. Sleep. Sit and learn.

I wait.

I wait and wait.

Five years of pretending her words were true.

Then I stop pretending, pry my window open and run away.

I take to the streets with the gems I learned: always watch your back, rely only on yourself, and most importantly— women can't be trusted.

NOW I'VE BEEN SADDLED with a bride who deals in trickery and deception, too.

"Trace her phone!" I boom to Dima and Nikolai as I come out.

"Oh fuck, really?" Dima says. "I'm sorry, Maxim. I thought she was in there." He squares his shoulders off to his computer, and his fingers fly over the keys.

I want to shout and rail at them for losing my bride, but really I'm at fault. I should've stationed Oleg at the door like Ravil did when he captured Lucy. I didn't want her to feel like a prisoner, but she's already proven herself a runner.

Hopefully she's just out shopping with my credit card. Proving to me and herself she's not a prisoner, and she can do what she wants.

"*Blyat*." Dima curses in Russian. "She's in Los Angeles. I'm sending the tracker to your phone."

Los Angeles.

Again, fuck me. That was where she went to college. She probably went to visit her friends. Or her old haunts.

I kick myself for not knowing more about her. I should have visited her when she was in college in the States. But I had no interest in tangling with her again. Not when she'd fucked me over so badly.

Besides, despite being kicked out of Igor's cell, I still belonged to him. Which meant she was still considered way off-limits. Not that I had an interest in seducing her.

Or being seduced.

And I knew from experience that even a friendly visit to her could go way off the rails.

Dammit. Looks like I'm going to L.A.

I'm sure she loves this game of chase.

Well, she's going to discover there are consequences to playing the brat.

I pack a quick bag and put my pistol in a gun case to be checked.

"You want us to go along?" Nikolai asks.

"No. She is my problem. I can deal with her."

The idea gives me a slight surge of satisfaction. Punishment might be just what we need. I'm a dominant man in bed. I know how to inflict a little pain with pleasure. I could certainly make Sasha pay in a way that's a win for both of us. Break down her walls and make her beg for satisfaction from me.

Maybe I have too much confidence, but I believe once she surrenders to me sexually, our battle of wills will cease. Right now, her walls are up too high. As long as she refuses to receive pleasure from me, she can continue to fight.

I grab a cab to the airport and get on the next flight out to Los Angeles.

~

SASHA

. . .

"THE RUSSIAN IS IN THE HOUSE!" I holler when Kayla throws the door wide for me. Just seeing the short, perky blonde makes me happy.

I prance past her and into the apartment like the queen returning to her castle. It looks very much the same—the bright red sofa and armchairs I bought with my father's credit cards, the rug under the coffee table. Even the paintings on the walls are the ones I hung.

I didn't buy my friends—at least I don't see it that way. They gave me so much—but we did live completely off Igor's money senior year. My friends enjoyed the free ride and, in exchange, opened their hearts and world to me.

"Don't prance past me without a hug!" Kayla chides, giving me a girly slap on my butt. I turn, and she throws herself at me, squeezing hard. "I missed you so much."

Ashley and Sheri are right behind her. "I can't believe you're here! How long can you stay?" Sheri asks. They are also degrees of blonde—it is California, after all—amplified with expensive highlights. Both could be models. When the four of us went out on the town together, we attracted massive attention.

A tall brunette I don't recognize clears her throat pointedly.

"This is Kimberly," Kayla says. "I met her doing dinner theatre. She took your room."

"But not my place in your heart," I say immediately, striking an old-time Hollywood actress pose.

"Never," Sheri laughs. "So how long, girl? Do you have a place to stay? You can sleep in my room if you want."

"I doubt I will stay the night. I ran away from my keeper, and he will probably catch up with me," I say ruefully. "Hopefully not before we get to party."

"Oh my God, you are so bad!" Ashley smacks my arm. "You gave Daddy's bodyguards the slip again?"

I wasn't under guard while I was at school—not like I was at home. But every once in a while, I'd catch a guy in familiar black tattoos following me. Taking photos to send to my dad. My friends and I used to toy with them, running over to throw ourselves at them, sit in their laps or lick their necks. Just to make them uncomfortable and throw the balance off. It was fun. I played that game on my own before, but my friends made it into more of a tournament. It became our goal to make my watchers squirm.

"Well, this time Daddy didn't put a bodyguard on me." I hold up my left hand. "He arranged a marriage."

"Oh shit," Ashley murmurs.

"What? Seriously?" Kayla sputters. "How does that work? Why?"

"What's the deal?" Sheri prods.

"So he died last week. And I guess he didn't feel comfortable leaving me with his fortune without a man to control it. So I had to marry this guy or inherit nothing."

"You have *got* to be kidding me," Kimberly says in a low voice. I don't even know her, but I appreciate her sympathy. "Are you okay? That is so intense."

"I'm so sorry, Sasha," Kayla says, turning her big, baby-doll brown eyes on me. "That's insane. And I'm sorry about your dad dying, too," she adds as an afterthought.

I shrug. "Yeah. I'm more upset about the marriage part, too." I know there's some grief over my dad, too, but it's so tainted I can't experience it.

"So is he Russian? Why are you here?" Sheri wants to know.

"He's Russian but he lives in Chicago. His name is Maxim."

"Is he old and ugly?"

I smirk. "Not old." I shake my head, thinking of Maxim's handsome face. The GQ way he dresses and carries himself, only the tattoos belying his poor upbringing. "Not ugly, either."

"How is he in bed?" Kimberly asked.

I shake my head. "I've been holding out on him."

"Still?" Kayla demands. She and my former roommates know I never had sex with men when I lived with them. I gave head frequently because I liked the power it gave me over a man, but I never let anyone into my panties. I never told my roomies I was a virgin, though. They may have guessed, but I liked to pretend the opposite.

"Do you actually hate men?" Ashley demands.

I shrug again. "I just don't think this guy should get control of my inheritance and my body without me having any choice in the matter. And since I can't do anything to change the inheritance part..."

"You're holding out," Kimberly finishes.

"But what about your needs?" Kayla said. "I think it's a mistake to think of sex as something only men get something out of. I mean, God knows, sometimes that's true, especially with college men, but you find yourself a real man? They know how to work for it."

"Mmm hmm," Sheri concurs.

"Yeah, he keeps promising I'll be satisfied," I admit.

"So make him *work*!" she encourages. "You should be getting more out of this arrangement."

"Hmm. Maybe." They may be right, but I have this shadowy fear that once I give my virginity up to Maxim he'll own me completely.

And despite the fact that I did save my virginity for my husband, just as my father had ordered, now that the time has come, I don't think he deserves it. Like my very virginity is some treasure he should've had to earn.

I was so willing to give it up to him once. But he spurned me.

He lost his chance.

C H A P T E R 8

 *axim*

AFTER CHECKING INTO CHATEAU MARMONT, Hollywood's famous boutique hotel, known for keeping celebrities' most scandalous secrets, I keep my eye on Sasha's tracker. I checked my credit card charges, and they match with the trip to L.A.—she didn't just give her phone to someone to give me the slip.

No, I imagine Sasha knows full well I will track her here and bring her back home; she just wants to make me work.

And to have her fun in the meantime.

According to Dima, the address she's been for the past couple hours is an apartment near USC—the same one she lived in last year. It seems she's visiting someone—a room-mate, perhaps.

A lover?

The idea unsettles me. More than unsettles me. It kicks me in the gut.

I never asked her if she was previously involved. Maybe she had a boyfriend in Moscow on the day we married. Maybe that's why she hated leaving.

No, that didn't seem right. She was hurt and angry over the marriage not heartbroken.

But the possibility of her having a past lover living in Los Angeles sits like a brick in my gut. I don't like the sense of jealousy it produces.

My fingers clench into fists. If Sasha's going to play this game with me, I will cut her loose. She can go back to Moscow with a target on her back. Take her chances on her own. I'm not going to play it with her.

Her marker moves. I watch until it stops and then zoom in. The Colony. It's a popular Hollywood nightclub. Irrational jealousy still tearing at my throat, I call for a car and take it to the club, flashing a crisp one hundred dollar bill to skip to the front of the line that's wrapped around the block.

The place is packed with beautiful people everywhere, bodies twining to pulsing music. I search the place for a particular redhead, fully ready to haul her out of there and show her the whip, but when I finally find her, my fury drains.

She's not with a man.

She's in a skin-tight red halter dress, sitting with a group of equally beautiful and scantily dressed young women. Probably her friends or roommates from college. They're out on the town, having a good time, as beautiful young women should. As Sasha should, if she were a normal twenty-three year old.

One who isn't an oil heiress in the Russian bratva with a hundred criminals after her fortune.

What stops me completely, though, is the smile that lights up her face. The group of them are sitting in a round booth, drinking cosmopolitans and laughing. Sasha appears completely at ease. At home. Her face is open and relaxed—full of life and joy.

It's so different from the haughty, closed visage she's given me since the day of our marriage. I'm suddenly ripped by guilt. Not that I think any of this shit is my fault—it's Igor's, without a doubt. But I feel sorry for Sasha and the position she's been put in.

I'm sorry for myself, too, for being saddled with the responsibility of keeping her alive. Her money isn't enough to sweeten the package. I was doing fine here without it. Ravil's made millions in real estate, and I've started to build my own wealth as well. Nothing like Sasha's or Ravil's, but enough for me. If I hadn't felt such a strong obligation to Igor, such a loyalty, I would've told him to find some other sucker.

I find a place to stand near the bar across the room. Somewhere I can watch to make sure Sasha and her friends are safe but where I won't be noticed by her. I order a shot of Beluga and watch. I've been checking the surroundings since I arrived, looking for anything that looks off. Any man with tattoos like mine, anyone watching my wife.

Wife. That word still feels foreign to me.

I don't notice any threats.

A song comes on that makes them all light up with what appears to be a shared memory. There's shouting and laughter, and they drain their drinks to get up and dance. I have to listen for a moment to recognize it. It's the dance-mix version of "Chandelier" by Sia.

The young women undulate and move with the music, and their beauty and obvious enjoyment draws attention from the sharks around them. Men move in from all sides.

I grit my teeth but stay where I am. I'll let her have her fun for now. As long as no one—

Oh, fuck no.

The moment some guy lays his hands on her hips, I'm out of my chair.

~

SASHA

AFTER DINNER at our favorite taco joint, my friends and I hit a club for dancing. I wear a tiny red dress and stilettos that I'd thrown in my giant purse. Out on the dance floor with my friends, I'm having the time of my life despite the sense of a ticking bomb about to go off.

Maxim hasn't called or texted, which probably means he's on his way or is already here. I have zero doubt he'll catch up to me, which is why I intend to enjoy the hell out of myself until he does.

I'm tipsy, so it takes me a minute to notice that some asshole put his hands on my hips from behind. I'm about to tell him to step back when Maxim suddenly appears in front of me.

It only takes one glance to know he's *pissed*. Not irritated, like he is going to throw me over his shoulder and carry me out, but lethally pissed.

I often forget, purposely, that my father's men are killers.

I literally gulp.

"Get him off you, or his blood will be on your hands." He speaks in Russian, so only I will understand.

I could elbow the guy away from me, but before the

thought even forms, I arrive at a better solution. I surge forward and wrap my arms around the neck of the enemy. Maybe it's the cocktails talking. Maybe it's out of a sheer survival instinct. They say women don't do flight or fight— we tend and befriend. Well, I'm bonding with my executioner.

It's not a hug. I absolutely mold my body to his, gluing my hips against his legs, riding one of his thighs like a cowgirl on a bull, still undulating to the music. My breasts press against his ribs, my lips brush his neck.

He instantly bands one strong arm around me, his palm splaying at my lower back then dropping lower to cup my ass and help me ride his leg. After a few seconds, I sense the fury in him dissipate. His body softens against mine. He sways to the music. "That's better," he murmurs in English.

Thank fuck. I realize I'm trembling, and most of my intoxication has disappeared with the adrenaline. For a moment there, I thought it was me he wanted to throttle. But it wasn't—it was the dickwad hitting on me.

At least, I hope so. I don't sense the dangerous aggression in him anymore.

Knowing he's dangerously possessive of me shouldn't give me flutters of excitement, but it does. Part of me loves that he showed up to claim me. And I'm probably pushing my luck—I'm definitely pushing my luck, but considering how nice it is to be dancing with him, I don't want to leave yet.

I'm sure he came to throw me back on a plane. I fully expect he'll tie me to his bed when we return. Oh damn, that thought turns me on.

But it is so incredibly wonderful to be with my friends again. I feel more like myself than I have in a year. With my girlfriends, I can be myself and laugh and have fun.

"Maxim," I begin, sounding breathless. "Can we, please… stay just a little longer?"

He circles his hips, taking mine on a ride around the park on his leg. I'm pretty sure my panties are soaked. I'm probably going to leave a wet spot on his leg. "Yes, we can stay," he says, swaying us side to side. "I didn't come all this way not to meet your American friends."

I let out an exhale of disbelief. I didn't expect him to be so accommodating.

But then he says, "I have all day tomorrow to punish you."

I probably should be worried, and I am—a little. But mostly the flutter in my belly is from excitement. Maybe it's because of the dark velvety purr in his voice when he mentions it.

I dare to lift my face to his and steal a peek at his expression. It's hard to read. He stares down at me with an unfathomable dark gaze. Maybe a hint of indulgence.

I stand on my tiptoes and move my lips against his. It's a tentative kiss. Not like my usual cock-tease shit. A real kiss—scary and sensual.

He doesn't kiss me back, just lets me do my thing, which makes it even more excruciating. I'm used to being the one men try to kiss. The one refusing or accepting the kiss. Not the one putting herself out there, hoping the gesture will be received. The vulnerability of it stings.

I ease away, and he stares down at me. "Is that your apology?" he asks.

I nod.

He brushes my cheek with the backs of his knuckles. His other hand still has firm hold of my ass, like he's showing every man here I belong to him. "It's good," he murmurs and lowers his mouth to mine in the same slow, exploratory way I kissed him. His lips slide over mine. He tastes like peppermint and vodka.

When I slide my tongue into his mouth, his dick lengthens against my belly.

"I have something for you," he says when the kiss ends. He slips a hand into his pocket.

I don't know what I expected—a pair of handcuffs? A ruler to slap my knuckles? A collar to attach a leash to?—but it's a small ring box. He picks up my left hand and slides my father's ring off my finger, then drops it loose into his pocket like it's nothing more significant than a coin. I wait, the anticipation of the moment leaving me breathless.

I'm still trembling—whether it's from my fear over his sudden appearance or the kiss or the ring he's about to give me, I can't be sure. He cracks open the box and takes out a big, beautiful ring.

Delicate but enormous, if that makes any sense. The center emerald is huge and beautiful, but the band is thin and covered in the same tiny diamonds that frame the emerald.

He slides it on my finger, and it fits perfectly. I'm not sure how he pulled that off. "Do you like it?"

I nod up at him. I think under different circumstances I might have pretended not to—I wouldn't have wanted to give him that win. But he's caught me by surprise. He showed up, as I expected, but didn't make a scene or even throw a punch at the guy touching me. And instead of ranting and railing and exacting punishment, he produces a beautiful wedding ring.

A thoughtful, expensive gift that I will actually enjoy wearing. It suits me, and, honestly, I love it.

"What is this?" Ashley grabs my hand and holds it up for the others to see. They squeal and gather up tightly around us.

"Is that your wedding ring?" Kayla demands.

"Is this Maxim?" Sheri asks at the same time.

"Will you join us in a toast?" Maxim asks. He's so damn suave—so slick. I sort of hate him for it because I've fallen victim to his charm in the past. But I also love it because he turned it on for my friends who matter very much to me. It's not that I need them to like him—I already filled them in on the whole medieval arranged marriage tale—but I want them to see what I'm up against.

Maybe I wouldn't mind if they liked him.

He leads us off the dance floor. Of course our booth has been taken, but Maxim lifts a hundred dollar bill held between his knuckles and a cocktail waitress instantly finds us. The same one who took forty-five minutes to make it to our table when we were sitting there before.

"A bottle of Moet and six glasses."

The waitress creams her panties over him. Or maybe it's just his money, but either way, she beams brighter than a thousand watt bulb and invites us to a corner of the bar where she uncorks and delivers the champagne in a chiller with ice. She starts to pour, but Maxim smoothly takes over, lifting his chin with his sexy-sauve grin to dismiss her.

She bats her lashes and disappears, telling him to just call her if he needs anything else. He catches her arm, and she leans back in as he asks for something else, and I grit my teeth. Maybe I'm as possessive as Maxim.

"To my beautiful bride," Maxim says after he pours the champagne into the six glasses and hands them out.

"Congratulations to you both," Kayla says.

"To you both," the others agree.

"*Na Zdorovie*," I say, reminding my friends of the Russian version of *cheers*.

"*Nostrovia!*" they all chant back—even Kimberly. The

others must've taught it to her, which makes me smile—my presence was honored and remembered.

Maxim catches my eye, and my belly flutters. "*Na Zdorovie*." He clinks my glass. He drains his glass and uses it to gesture to us. "Tell me—how do you all know each other? You are all actresses?"

Kayla smiles. "I am." She tosses an arm around my shoulder. "We were in theatre together all four years. And we met these two doing promotions our junior year." She indicates Sheri and Ashley. "We all lived together senior year. And this one is our replacement-Sasha." She lifts her chin at Kimberly. "She's our new roommate and also works for the promotion company."

"There's no replacing Sasha," I say, spilling a few drops of my champagne as I hold my arms up for them to admire my figure. "No offense, of course." I wink at Kimberly, even though I'm certain she knows I'm kidding.

"What promotions?" Maxim looks puzzled.

"We dressed up in skimpy costumes to promote new products at launches." I shrug. "Like for new alcohol or energy drinks or meal replacement bars. It paid cash and was good fun."

"I'll bet you had fun." This time I'm sure I detect indulgence in Maxim's gaze. "A round of shots?"

Why is he being so nice to me?

It puts me on edge, waiting for the hammer to drop.

"Hell, yes!" my friends shout, and Maxim lifts another hundred dollar bill in the air to get us instant service.

"Six shots of Cazador tequila. With salt and lime."

"Tequila!" my friends cheer. Their happiness is infectious. It makes me relax and forget my anxieties over Maxim.

It costs more than the hundred dollar bill, and he pulls out his wallet for another. While he's talking to the cocktail waitress, Ashley mouths the words, *he's hot.*

I steal a glance, irrationally proud that my friends think so.

He *is* hot. He's in a crisp designer button-down, open at the collar, looking California-perfect. Like he'd known he'd be coming to a posh nightclub. But this is how he always dresses—at least in the week since we've been married.

"I like him," Kayla says out loud, leaning forward over the bar conspiratorially.

"I like him for you," Sheri concurs, pointing at me. She waggles her brows. "Make him work. I'll bet he's good."

Maxim's attention returns, and my friends all grin mischievously. He takes it all in with a smirk. "I'll bet you ladies get into all kinds of trouble." His gaze slides sideways, and he suddenly tugs my hand. "Come on, a table opened up."

We launch into action to claim a perfect circular booth like the one we had before. Another group tries to move in at the same time but Maxim turns to face them, blocking them with his body.

"No way, buddy." One of the guys in their group starts to give him shit. "We've been waiting for this table."

I loop my arm through his and speak to the guy. "Don't fuck with the Russian," I say, letting my accent come out thickly. "He will clean the floor with you."

Maxim doesn't move. He doesn't speak. He just stares at the guy with an intensity that could cut glass.

"Come on." The women with the would-be hero tug him away.

I slide into the booth with my friends, and Maxim takes the end seat, our protector.

"You do love drama, don't you, *caxapok*?" He appears unruffled.

The criticism hits a little too close to home—it was what my father always accused me of—needing attention. Being a drama queen. "What?"

"Nothing. Just know when you get involved like that, you double the chances of me hurting someone."

"How's that?"

My friends are listening, and I get uneasy, thinking this might not be something I should air in front of them.

Maxim appears amused, though. He gives an easy shrug. "Because if they say something disrespectful to you, I *have to* kill them."

My friends *ooh* over his comment. I guess it is sort of swoon-worthy. Especially if you don't know he probably means *literally kill*.

I'm saved from responding by the arrival of our cocktail waitress—or I should say *his* because she is definitely all about him.

She sets a shot glass of tequila in front of each of us, along with a small plate of lime wedges and the salt shaker.

Maxim reaches for the salt shaker, beating me to it. "Body shots. I pick the location."

I blink at him. I know what body shots are. I've done them before with stupid college boys. But never with the hot, virile man beside me. The guy I'm married to. The man my friends and the liquor I've already consumed has lowered my inhibitions.

I hesitate, waiting to see where he'll put the salt, but he chooses an innocuous place—the webbing between his thumb and forefinger. He licks it and sprinkles on the salt, then holds the lime in his teeth.

All the while, my friends watch, waiting to do their shots for the entertainment at hand to unfold.

He brings his hand to my lips. I lick, pound my shot and bite into the lime between his lips as my friends whoop and holler.

"Are you sharing, girl? Because I might want to lick some of that, too," Kimberly says with a wink.

I know she's kidding—probably swaying it to nudge me into having sex with Maxim, but I can't deny the smack of jealousy that hits me square in the chest. It's that, along with my newly-recognized exhibitionism, that makes me grab a lime and the salt shaker. "Come and get it, big boy." I rub the lime across the top of one of my breasts where the skin shows above the dress, then sprinkle salt on top. I shoot him a *do-you-dare?* look, even though I have zero doubt he does, indeed, dare.

Yes, he makes a total show out of it, and I'm the center of attention—exactly the way I like it. He moves in slowly and drags his tongue across the salt. Then he swipes again, and a third time, before dipping his tongue below the top of my dress and teasing my nipple.

"Mmm." He comes up and holds my gaze while he downs the tequila. He doesn't suck the lime in my teeth. Instead, he kisses the fuck out of my mouth, twisting and torquing the lime between our lips while holding the back of my head captive.

When he finally stops, I spit the lime onto the table and gasp for breath.

Kayla fans herself. "Oh my gawd. So that's how it's done."

"Your turn." Maxim winks, and my friends salt their own thumbs and down their shot.

A round of bottled waters magically appears—Maxim

must've ordered them before the cocktail waitress left the last time.

"Let's go dance," I suggest, somewhat drunkenly after I've downed half my water.

Maxim stands to let me out. "You want me to go with you or stay here and hold the table?"

I put my hands on his chest, accidentally bumping right up against him when I lose my balance. Why was he being so dang nice to me?

Oh damn, I asked that out loud. I definitely need to dance off that tequila shot.

I go up on my tiptoes and press a sloppy kiss on his lips. "Thank you for saving our table," I say and weave onto the floor with Kayla and Ashley. The other two stay behind with Maxim. I whirl when I get a few steps away and point between them. "No body shots on him while I'm away. He's mine."

Maxim's amused smile sends cascades of warmth into my belly and down my inner thighs.

Handsome husband.

 *axim*

MY BRIDE and her friends like the attention they garner on the dance floor. I'm a possessive man—extremely possessive. And when that *mudak* had his hands on her, I was jealous as hell. But I'm not one of those guys who needs his woman to cover up and not show off the gifts God gave her. Especially not if it gets her horny flaunting it.

The women dance and return. I push water, then order another round of cocktails, which they don't finish. The next time they go out to dance I go with them. There are two-foot platforms people can climb onto to dance against the wall, and I lead the group back there. I hold Sasha's hand to steady her and lift my chin toward the platform. There are people dancing on it, but I project enough authority—like I own the place, and I decide who gets to dance on the mini stages—that the people on it decide to hop down.

Sasha loves it. She climbs on and pulls her friends up.

Twirling and bouncing with pleasure. She looks down at me with the heat of alcohol-induced lust and exhibitionism in her eyes. "Are you coming up?" she calls down over the music.

I shake my head. "I'm standing guard."

Her friends love that. They whoop and ooh. I didn't say it for effect, though. I am literally standing guard. From where I dance, I get flashes of panty beneath their short skirts, and any guy who takes that as a green light to approach is going to catch my knuckles in his gut.

There's an art to knowing when to leave a party when alcohol is involved. You want to leave just past its peak, while everything is still perfect and fun, but you're not too inebriated.

I watch until their exuberance starts to wilt, and then I swoop them down off the platform and outside to get some fresh air. Once they cool off, I suggest it's time to go.

Sasha collects her big purse from the coat check, and I put her friends in the first cab waiting in front of the elite club. I walk around to the driver's window and hand him a hundred dollar bill. "This is for their ride. If they don't get home safely, I will hunt you down and kill you."

Sasha smacks my arm as the cab driver bobs his head and accepts the cash.

"You can't say that."

"I can," I counter. "I did." I claim a second cab for us.

Sasha shakes her head. She's somewhere between tipsy and sloshed, so all her movements are exaggerated and slow. "Because you're a man you can throw your weight around like that. There's no way I could ever r-reenact that scene and have the cabbie take me seriously." I catch her elbow as she wobbles on the pavement, then hand her into the back of the cab and follow her in.

"Chateau Marmont," I tell the driver.

Sasha's still chewing on the injustice. "I don't think I could even get that cocktail waitress to give me decent service. And it's *my* money you're throwing around."

"It was my own," I correct her.

"Either way, you still have all the power. I have none."

Getting into a philosophical discussion with her in this state is probably a bad idea, but I do, anyway. She's right— playing alpha male is easy when you are one, but she sees herself as far more weak than she is. "Power isn't just something divvied out by gender. And it's *definitely* not something that's bestowed on you by others. It's a choice you make for yourself. Either you react to everyone else, or you claim your own power."

"Right. How do you think I should've taken my own power when my dad called me in to tell me to marry you or lose my inheritance? Hmm? Should I have told him to go fuck himself? Is that what you would've done?"

She has a point.

But so do I.

"No, Sasha. But you're married to me now, and you have a choice. You can keep pushing and prodding me—running away and making me chase—to try to get the power from me. Or you can decide you're my equal and make your demands. Tell me what you need from me to make this work."

She blinks at me, wide-eyed, silent for a moment. Then she says, "But I don't want it to work."

Her words hit me like a cement block to my head.

"What's the alternative, *caxapok*? We divorce, and the money goes to Vladimir? Or we separate, and one of your father's men either kidnaps or kills you for your fortune?"

"I did make my demands." She smacks my arm with the back of her hand. "I asked you to let me stay in Moscow. And how did that go over for me? Hm? Oh yeah, I remember, it ended with you carrying me out to the car like a sack of potatoes!"

My lips twitch at the memory and at her feistiness. "My ability to keep you alive is possibly the sole reason your father picked me. Leaving you in Moscow wouldn't accomplish that."

"Okay, so I demanded my own bedroom. What did that get me?"

The taxi pulls up in front of our hotel. I pay him, and he opens Sasha's door for her. I walk around to take her hand.

"I didn't trust you not to run away. And with good reason, apparently."

"Are you really just talking about sex here when you tell me to demand what I need?" Sasha asks as we step into the lobby.

I put my finger over her lips with a smile because she's too loud, and she giggles.

"Is that it?" she asks again as I guide her down the hallway. "You want me to demand sex? My friends think I should."

I open our room, and she looks around, just now noticing her surroundings. "Where are we?"

"Chateau Marmont."

She turns around and opens her arms. "I've always wanted to stay here."

I step closer, my hands lightly touching her waist. "And now you have."

She totters, blinking. It's probably wrong to try to seduce my wife when she's been drinking, but I've been hard as concrete since she first threw herself at me on the dance floor.

"How would you demand it?" I prompt, sliding my hands down her hips until I get to the very short hemline of her dress. I inch it up.

"See, the thing is, I don't think you deserve it," she says to me.

On the other hand, her tipsiness makes this a perfect time to figure out what schemes are going on in that beautiful head of hers.

"You're right," I agree. "I don't deserve it. Not after you offered yourself up so prettily before, and I didn't accept." As I speak, I slowly hike her dress up over her ass, then up her torso and over her head.

There. It's out in the open. Maybe we can put this behind us once and for all.

She's stunning in a pink bra and matching thong. Curvy, voluptuous, and perfect.

Sasha's composure crumbles a little, probably both at being stripped and by the reminder. But being my fiery beautiful bride, she pops open her own bra, allowing her breasts to spring free and bounce. She's double D's all the way and fucking gorgeous with her pale skin and pink nipples. She drops the bra on the floor, lifts her chin and cups her pretty breasts proudly. "Well, this is what you missed out on, Max. And you don't get a second chance."

"Sasha, I wanted you then, and I want you now." I step into her space, unbuttoning my shirt and tossing it to the floor. "If you weren't seventeen and the *pakhan's* daughter, I would've been on you all night, every night on that trip." I tug off my undershirt. "Believe me."

She sets her jaw like she doesn't want to believe me, but I know I have her attention. I'm saying the right thing, for once.

I take a chance and lightly touch her waist. Let my fingers slip under the waistband of her thong. I don't move it. It's just a suggestion of what I might do. "Sugar, your father would've killed me. And not a nice, swift mercy killing. He would've cut off my balls. Cut off every finger that touched you. And then slit my throat and listened to me beg as I bled out."

She shakes her head and rolls her pouty lips inward. Instead of retreating, though, she leans into me, her nipples brushing against my bare chest. "You didn't just refuse me. You went and *told my father*." She smacks my chest. The accusation and betrayal in her eyes slices into me. Especially when a sheen of tears coats her eyes. "You know what he did?" She tries to shove me away, but I don't move. "He slapped my face and called me a whore." She slaps mine.

Aw, fuck. My heart twists for her. Igor was a fucking loser as a father to her. I cup her cheek as if I can soothe away the sting of the years' old slap.

"No one will ever slap your face again—this I promise you. Not if they want to live."

She blinks rapidly.

"Fuck, sugar. I'm sorry. I'm so sorry. But I had to tell him." I let my hands settle on her hips for real and gently maneuver her backward toward the bed. "Igor was so twisted, I was afraid it was a test. Like he told you to tempt me to find out if I was loyal. If I respected his law. And even if it wasn't a test, if anyone else on that yacht told him they'd seen you going in or out of my cabin, I'd have been a dead man. It wasn't something I could wait to be accused of—I had to be proactive. You put my head on the chopping block coming in that room."

I stop guiding her before the backs of her legs hit the mattress. I want to get her horizontal, but this conversation is too important to rush through. I should've had it with her the day we married.

"I don't forgive you," she says sulkily, and I sense the lie.

"Give me a do-over," I entreat. "The way I remember it, you were in the middle of my bed." I lift her hips to plop her down on the bed. "Only you weren't wearing these." I reach for the thong, going slowly in case she protests.

She doesn't. Her pupils are wide as she reclines on her elbows and watches me drag the scrap of fabric down her legs.

She isn't waxed bare, but has a neat auburn trim. Her belly shudders in and out.

"Beautiful," I murmur. "You were beautiful then, but you're even more beautiful now."

"What's different?" Her voice is husky.

I push her knees up, spreading them wide and settle between her legs. "Now I can have you."

She tries to snap them shut around my ears. "I didn't say that."

I lick into her, and she gasps, tightening her thighs even more. I grasp her legs and stroke my palm up and down one of them. "I didn't mean it that way. Only that you're an adult and Igor's dead." The truth is, I didn't even let myself look at her the night I found her in my room. I mean, I saw, but I forced my mind to ignore what I saw. I didn't even sprout a chub because I knew it would be wrong.

So wrong.

I ease her knees back open and tongue her, tracing around her pink bits, then sucking her clit between my lips.

I try to work my index finger inside her, but she's tight as hell. She whimpers slightly. When I look up to read her face, I find her expression slightly alarmed.

Goosebumps shoot out on my arms as it hits me—my bride might be a virgin after all.

"W-weren't you going to punish me?" Her cheeks flush—whether it's excitement or embarrassment I can't be sure.

I know she's diverting my attention, but I fucking love that she asked. It's the second time she's reminded me of her punishment. I'm thinking she loves the idea as much as I do. Punishment probably seems safer to her now than letting me conquer that pussy of hers—especially if she's a virgin like I'm starting to suspect.

I smirk. "I was going to wait until morning when you were sober, but if you want your spanking now, I'm happy to deliver."

I don't give her a chance to respond, I just tuck my hand under one side of her hips to roll her to her belly. She spreads her legs a little, like a good girl. I give her ass a few smacks and rub.

Fuck. Sasha *is* a good girl. She may play bad girl all day long, but at the end of it all, she kept this pussy pristine because Igor told her to lock it up. She fooled me. She fooled everybody. But the sex-tease act was a manipulation. Underneath it all, my bride is an innocent.

She even fooled Igor because he flat-out stated she wasn't a virgin.

He was an ass.

I dip my fingers between her soft thighs and rub. Her pussy weeps, greedy for attention. I spread the moisture up to circle her clit and back again. Then I deliver several hard smacks. "That's for letting that *mudak* touch you," I tell her, using the Russian word for *asshole* instead of the English. "That is the part I won't be quick to forgive." I stroke again, teasing her entrance with the tip of my finger before working it inside.

She spreads her legs wider, tipping her ass back to give me better access. "I was about to give him the elbow when you arrived."

I slowly pump my finger as I slap her ass a few times with my free hand. "That better be fucking true."

She moans. "It is." Her accent's grown thicker.

I ease out of her and warm her ass again with another flurry of spanks. I start light and gradually increase the power behind the spanks until she starts to squirm and reach back. I clasp her wrist and bend her arm behind her back. "That's for making me get on a fucking plane to chase you." I slap the backs of her legs, and she cries out, cursing me in Russian. Her porcelain skin glows pink with my handprints, and I can't deny the surge of possessiveness I experience admiring it.

I slide my middle finger between her legs at the same time my thumb dips between her cheeks to nudge her back pucker. She squeezes her ass cheeks up tight against the intrusion.

I slap her ass with my free hand and continue to work my middle finger past her tight entrance and apply pressure with my thumb. I prod her cheeks open and drop a little saliva between them to aid my progress.

"What are you—*oh*!" Sasha gasps as I breach her back hole, too. She pants, her hips rocking to take my middle finger deeper. I lean on my shin beside her, to get in close, working my digits in both her holes. I alternate, filling her pussy, then her ass as she writhes and moans incoherently. I work my free hand under her hips to find her clit and she bucks, opening her legs even wider. She's beautiful—fully surrendered, yielding, responsive. I try to get a second finger inside her tight entrance while I circle her clit.

"Maxim." She sounds alarmed. She must be close to orgasm.

"That's right, *caxapok*." *Say my fucking name*. I'm simultaneously shocked by how far we've come since yesterday and stunned at how right it feels. How satisfying it is to hear my reluctant bride croak my name in that desperate, needy tone.

I pump into both holes simultaneously, and she pushes

RENEE ROSE

back to take me deeper, arching her back. My cock strains hard against my zipper, but now that I suspect she's a virgin, I can't take her. Not tonight when she's been drinking. It would be wrong—even if she is my wife.

"Maxim—*Gospodi.*" She clenches both holes, drawing my digits deeper as she comes with a strangled cry. I continue to rub her clit until her muscles stop squeezing and pulsing. Until she sinks back into the bed, all the tension in her body releasing.

I lean over and bite her shoulder, then kiss the center of her back. "Good girl. You took your punishment so well, sugar." I ease my fingers out and go to the bathroom to wash up and bring her a damp washcloth. She's already half-sleep, the alcohol and her orgasm sending her off into dreamland. I manage to get her under the covers and then undress, turn off the light, and crawl in beside her.

She's completely naked and right beside me.

Every part of me wants to roll her over and fuck her until the bed breaks, but somehow I manage to keep a leash on my lust.

I settle instead for spooning my glorious, naughty bratva princess and cupping her dripping wet pussy possessively.

"This pussy is mine," I growl into her ear, even though she's mostly asleep. I stroke her swollen, slick sex. "It gets wet for me, doesn't it? Only for me."

Her breath catches a bit, and she stirs, pushing her backside against my straining cock.

"I'm the only man who will ever know how fucking sweet it is. How it feels when you're swollen and needy. How it tastes when you're trembling against my mouth."

She lets out a whimper-sigh.

"You were a good girl to save yourself for me."

Her breathing stops.

After a moment of holding it, she rolls over to face me, her hands finding my chest in the darkness. "How did you know?"

I gather her against my body, ignoring the powerful need to consummate our marriage. To pound between those milky thighs until she screams herself hoarse. "Am I right?"

She whimpers and tucks her face into my shoulder after a few moments, her breathing evens out again, and I realize she's fallen back to sleep.

It's answer enough. My bride is innocent.

Not for long, though.

I will pop that cherry before we return to Chicago.

CHAPTER 10

I WAKE NAKED in a room in Chateau Marmont with Maxim's longer body spooned behind mine, his hand palming my breast, his cock twitching against my ass.

Gospodi.

My face heats as the memories from last night flood in. How much of my true self I revealed—my hurt over his rejection. My *virginity*.

Ack!

Was that why he didn't have sex with me last night? Was he being a gentleman?

I realize with a squirmy feeling in my belly that I think that was exactly it.

And I don't like to think of Maxim as a gentleman. I want to keep believing he's the bad guy.

It makes things much easier.

Navigating a new forced marriage to a guy I actually want? A guy whose love I crave like my next breath?

That's a different story. One I could slip into so easily.

I don't want to become that needy, pathetic, desperate-for-attention teenager again. I fucking hate her.

So I flip the script. I can't wait in this bed, trembling like a flower to feel what it's like to have my virginity plucked by the husband my father forced on me. I'm not going to be the medieval princess! I turn in bed, pushing Maxim to his back with a hand on his inked chest.

His eyes snap open and lock onto mine, curiosity glinting there.

I'm used to him making the first move. He's the aggressor. I dodge and retreat. So for one second, out of habit, I wait for his reaction. I expect him to say or do something. To tell me to stop or go on. But his lids droop as he waits, and just like that, all the power flows to me.

To keep it, I have to pretend he's someone else—one of the college guys I plucked from a bar or one of my father's dumber soldiers. Some guy who lets me call all the shots. I trail my fingernail down his chest as I straddle him. I flick his nipple with my fingernail until it peaks while I crawl backward, taking the sheets with me.

His cock springs up in greeting. I grasp the base firmly and lower my mouth, watching his eyes darken. I flick the head of his cock with the tip of my tongue—just a tease.

A muscle ticks near Maxim's nose—like the start of a snarl, but then it quickly smooths. The sight of it makes my heart beat faster.

It's not Maxim. It's some boy-toy. Someone easy to play.

I squeeze the base of his dick and lick all around his mushroom head. A drop of pre-cum leaks from his slit, and I lick it off. I sense his impatience. He doesn't like the tease.

Or maybe he does—I can't tell. Maybe I'm just nervous. But I stop delaying and engulf as much of his cock as I can get into my mouth all at once.

He groans, fisting the sheets by his side.

Encouraged, I bob my head up and down over his straining member, listening to his breath grow ragged.

"That's it, sugar," he rumbles, gripping the back of my head and encouraging me to take him deeper.

He's back in command, but I keep showing off, suddenly rather desperate to show him I know what I'm doing. I give him my very best blow-job—and sucking men off is a skill I've developed well.

I massage his balls and his prostate with one hand while the other fist glides up and down over his cock to make up for the length I can't fit in my mouth. I swirl my tongue around, I suck hard. I alternate quick, short bobs over the head with taking him long and deep, into the pocket of my cheek and sometimes into the back of my throat.

His thighs flex beneath me, his groans of my name grow more frequent. His fist tangles in my hair, pulling at my scalp.

It's disrespectful—no man's ever done it to me before, and I half-hate it. But I half-love it, too. It's so Maxim—everything he is. Aggressive, bossy, confident. I'm turned on by it—more turned on than I've ever been giving a man pleasure before. *Way* more.

I work his cock like I want to please. I don't know if I'm trying to prove something or if I really do need to please the man. All I know is I suck so hard my jaw aches, and I don't stop, even when my eyes water from him hitting the back of my throat.

"Fuck, Sasha, *fuck*," he growls. "I'm going to come."

I don't pop off. I swallow like a good girl. I lick him

clean, and then I sit back on his thighs and wipe my mouth, watching him watching me.

"Sugar." He reaches for me, but I dismount from the bed and walk to the bathroom, letting my hips sway to show off my bare ass. I shut the door and start the shower, my heart pounding.

Shit. I'm so in over my head. My body is all hot and needy. I've never wanted to have sex so badly in my life. Part of me wishes I'd let Maxim pull me down beside him and do whatever it is he wanted to with me.

But there's another part of me freaking out.

Freaking *the fuck* out.

I don't even know what I'm freaking out about. I step into the shower and wash everywhere, like the soap and shampoo will somehow cleanse me of this gnawing anxiety.

And that's when it hits me: I can't do this with Maxim.

It's way too scary. Because if he doesn't hate me, if I stop refusing to sleep with him…

Then we're something else. We're my parents—the bratva boss and his woman.

I'm his wife not his mistress, but it's no different. Maxim is just like my father. And me? The very heart of me?

I fear I could be just as pathetic as my mother.

What if I'm as needy as she was? Waiting around for her man to throw her the scraps of his attention. Being at the ready to perform for him, to please him, from the moment he walked in the door until the moment he walked right back out. Her job was to look beautiful, satisfy him in bed and obey his orders.

She played the role to perfection, and he still didn't leave her with a dime. He literally gave her to his right-hand man, like she was a possession to be handed down.

Just like he gave me to Maxim.

So I'm not going to be like her. End of story. I'm not going to fall for Maxim and throw myself at his feet and wait for his scraps of attention. I will figure out how to live with him without losing my heart.

I turn the water off and climb out of the shower, taking my time drying off. I don't want to open the door and come out of the bathroom. I don't know if I'm ready to see Maxim —I'm not sure if I've steeled my heart enough. I hold the knob and lean my head against the door, heart thumping. But when I finally brace myself and open it, I find him asleep. The orgasm must've relaxed him back into slumber.

I tiptoe through the room and put on my travel clothes from yesterday and gather up my things. I know I can't run far. I know he'll find me immediately, whether it's a matter of minutes or hours. But I have to run.

I pick up my purse and open the door.

"One more step, and I'll turn your ass purple."

CHAPTER 11

 axim

SASHA FREEZES in place at my threat then closes the door.

She fucking played me.

Women. You can't trust them. They lie and manipulate. She just gave me the hottest blowjob in the history of all blowjobs, and I stupidly thought it meant we were getting somewhere.

But no. It was all a manipulation.

Damn her.

I sit up in the bed and swing my legs over the side. "Come here."

She lifts her chin. "I'm fine where I am, thank you."

My lips twitch, but I suppress my smile. I shouldn't be amused by her fear. Except it makes my cock lengthen, thoughts of elaborate sex-filled punishments floating into my brain and smoothing out my temper.

I pat the bed beside me. "Come here, *caxapok*," I coax. "I don't bite hard." I smirk. "Not you, anyway."

Her jaw flexes, but she drops her large purse and walks over to the bed like I asked.

She's a good girl at her core, I remind myself.

Or maybe not. I'd interpreted her virginity that way, but perhaps that's just another part of her feminine manipulations. She's never given herself to anyone because she doesn't share. She uses blowjobs to ensnare men into her web, but they never get the prize.

I grind my teeth.

"Where were you going?"

Her haughty spoiled girl expression comes into place as she opens her mouth, and I snap, "*Don't fucking lie*" before she gets a word out.

She closes her mouth again, flickers of fear and vulnerability in her expression.

"The truth," I insist. "Or maybe that was the wrong question. Maybe the right one is, *why* were you leaving?"

She blinks rapidly, looking away. Her full lips shape a pout, and I find I want to kiss the fuck out of them, remembering how they looked stretched around my cock. "I...I just needed some space," she admits with a sigh.

I'm torn between irritation and understanding.

"Space is a luxury neither of us have right now," I snap then rein in my impatience. "Listen to me. Your father just died. There's instability in the organization—massive instability. You inherited the biggest part of his wealth. I imagine there are dozens of men scheming about how to make a grab for that right now before the dust settles. Your father bound you to me for a number of reasons. One, marriage to me takes you out of the country, which makes it significantly harder to plot to kill you. Two, I know how to keep you safe. Many

THE FIXER

men in Moscow will remember my reputation." I draw a finger across the ink on my knuckles, a mark for every kill.

She sits unmoving, those pouting lips taunting me.

"I have Dima working on tracking everyone who comes into the country from Russia and cross-referencing them with known members of the brotherhood. He's writing a program for it now, but until that's in place and until we see how things shake out in Moscow, I need to keep eyes on you at all times. I'm sorry, sugar. I'm not thrilled with it, either."

Her gaze drops, and I sense her concession.

"Come here." I loop an arm around her waist and drag her to sit on my lap. She sits stiffly at first. I pick up her leg and open it wide, so it sits on the outside of my knee and trace my fingertips lightly up her inner thigh. She shivers, her buttocks tensing over my cock.

She's in another one of her body-hugging dresses—not the one she wore last night. This one is more casual, made of a soft, charcoal t-shirt material. It rolls up her thighs when I nudge it.

"I don't know if you're punishing me or you want to be punished, sugar, but you have to find another game. This one is too dangerous, *da*?"

She draws in a shaky breath. I do have an affect on her—that much I know. Last night, despite her very bold and in my face move of taking off for Los Angeles, she was nervous when I showed up. I sensed her trembling when she launched herself at me on the dance floor.

I continue to lightly tickle the inside of her thigh, tracing my fingers up and down, getting a little higher each time.

"Where were you going, Sasha?"

"I'm not ready to leave L.A.," she says. I feel the thrum of her wild heartbeat through her back.

"No?" I nuzzle her neck, brushing my lips against her

skin. "Then all you had to do was ask to stay. You think I could deny you anything after that life-altering blowjob you just gave me?"

"I shouldn't have to ask," she mumbles.

Before my temper flares, I remember how free and happy she looked last night with her friends. It's true. She should be out living her life the way she wants. Finding her own joy. "You shouldn't," I agree. "But that's not our reality. When things settle, I'll let the leash off—I promise. Until then, you'll work with me on this."

She squirms on my lap.

"We can stay another day." I let my finger brush the gusset of her panties, and her belly shudders in. "What did you want to do while we're here?"

"I want to see my friends again."

"Of course."

"And go to the beach. And shopping."

I slide my finger under her panties to brush over her soft flesh there. "I have a few items to shop for." I use a musing tone. "Things I need for your punishment. Implements to spank you with." Her ass tightens on my lap. "Things to put in your virgin ass. Some lube, so you can take my cock nice and deep. Rope to tie you up with."

I seem to have rendered her speechless. I'm not even sure she's breathing.

"Now turn around and give me one of those apologies you offered me last night."

She doesn't move for a few beats. Then her head turns slowly. She stands and rotates, straddles my lap. "Was it this?" There's a purr in her voice—but also enough vulnerability to keep me from annoyance with her act. After all, I asked her to perform it. She brings her lips to mine in what is

a very sweet kiss. Not timid, but not aggressive. Almost…
innocent.

I know she's not that innocent, but I suddenly wonder if
she's held her kisses back from other men, as well.

Many people who hate intimacy engage in sex without
kissing. My suitemate, Pavel, for example.

I kiss her back, holding her jaw to deepen it. She squirms
on my lap. I grab her ass with my other hand and yank her
hips over mine, so her core rubs over my hardening cock. She
rocks her pelvis, riding me.

When I ease back, she blinks at me, eyes dilated.

"It's time for your punishment."

Her gaze is a mixture of wariness and arousal.

I bring her hand to my lips and kiss it. "I'll make it brief,"
I promise. "And there will be a reward for your surrender."

My words have the opposite effect intended. Now she
really appears unsure. I imagine her pride makes surrender
less appealing than pain. I lower my head and bite her breast
through her dress. "This comes off." I'm already tugging the
dress over her head as I finish speaking.

She doesn't fight me. She still straddles my lap, slightly
sullen, slightly submissive.

Very sexy.

It sort of hits me for the first time.

This fuck-hot woman is *my wife*. She is the full package
in the looks department—blessed with a brick house body, a
movie star face, and gorgeous, thick natural auburn hair. She
could make it as an actress. Of course, her marriage to me
keeps her from that career.

She's full of life and vitality—sassy as hell. A total handful.

But most importantly—all mine.

This hot-tease woman is mine.

I nip at her breast through her bra as I unfasten it in the back. She rocks over my cock again in her tiny g-string. I kiss the front of her shoulder and then urge her to stand.

I pivot and plop a couple pillows in the center of the bed. "Panties off. Lie over the pillows."

Alarm flares in her eyes. "What are you going to do?"

I honestly haven't decided yet. I'm improvising. I walk around the room, noting my belt, which looks too thin and whippy. There's one of those plastic rods hanging from the curtains—the kind used to pull them open and closed. I detach it and smack it into my hand. It bites. It would make an impression.

She still hasn't climbed into position. I suspect she's ready to punch me in the nose and run if she doesn't like my answer.

"I'm going to give you three strokes with this rod. And then I'm going to fuck the living daylights out of you."

Her chest heaves with a breath, making her gorgeous tits shift.

I step in close—seductive, not stern. I brush her hair back and kiss her in the place where shoulder meets neck. "You saved yourself for me," I murmur, appreciatively.

She takes a half-step back. "Not for you."

"For me," I insist. "We both wanted each other then, and we both had to wait."

She inches closer to me, that same wary lust flickering in her eyes. "I didn't say I would have sex with you." She sounds breathless.

I step so close, her nipples contact my chest. My mouth hovers over hers. "I won't force you."

Her gaze searches mine.

I allow my lips to tilt upward. "I will punish you, though. The fucking is the reward." I let my hand lightly cup her ass.

She shivers and brings her hands to my chest like she's going to push me away, only she doesn't. "You're crass."

"Apologies."

"You're not sorry."

"Are you?" I cock a brow.

She shakes her head slowly.

"Hmm."

We're at an impasse. I can't decide if I should actually follow through with punishment—not without some clearer indication of consent. The other times she wanted to be spanked—she basically asked me for it.

"Surrender, Sasha," I coax.

She eyes the implement in my hand. "Only three?"

"I'll be gentle."

Another shiver runs through her, and she promptly climbs onto the bed.

Satisfaction makes my cock punch out straight. I test the rod a few times on my thigh to get the force right, then whip her once with it.

She lets out a squeal—the cutest fucking squeal I've ever heard in my life. Once again, a surge of pleasure rushes through me.

This is my wife.

She's mine.

I can elicit those squeals for the rest of my fucking life. All I have to do is convince her that marriage to me wasn't the worst thing that happened to her.

I rub out the sting of the first stripe and give her ass a gentle slap, then deliver another with the pseudo-cane.

She squeals again, her ass tightening, her heels kicking up into the air.

I catch one ankle and stroke down her calf. "You left your

heels on for me," I murmur appreciatively. "That's so fucking hot."

She looks over her shoulder at me.

"New rule. This is how you will always be punished—naked except for your heels."

"You're crazy," she says, but I hear the smile in her voice.

"You're hot. My very hot wife." I deliver the last stripe to get it over with, then knead and massage away the sting. I climb on the bed behind her to massage with both hands. "Good girl. Are you ready for your reward?"

I don't wait for her reply, I just push her legs open wide and pull her hips back to get my tongue on her sex. She's already dripping wet. I lick and suck at her labia, penetrate her with my tongue, then move up to rim her anus.

She lets out that squeal, and her anus flutters, but I hold her in place for the pleasure.

After a few moments, she starts moaning. A few more, and she's chanting in Russian. "Maxim...Maxim. What are you doing? *Gospodi*, it's so good."

"You ready for my cock, beautiful?"

I'm surprised when she answers, "Yes" without hesitation.

Her surrender alone is enough to make me come. I want to slam into her bareback, but even though I know I'm clean and she's a virgin, it wouldn't be right. She may be my wife, but she may not want a pregnancy.

I find a condom in my wallet and roll it on. When I come back I ready her again with my tongue first. "Up on your knees, sugar. Chest on the pillows."

I'm probably being a jackass. A woman's first time should probably be on her back, with her lover looking into her eyes. But we aren't that couple. Eye contact might be too much vulnerability between us. Rough and punitive is how she likes it. How I want to give it.

We don't have a fairytale marriage.

Not yet, anyway.

Maybe we'll get there.

With a wife this hot, I should work to get us there. I'm the fixer, after all. I can fix anything.

Even a wife who doesn't want me.

She climbs into position, proving my instincts right. I squeeze her ass as I line my cock up, stroke it over her entrance. She was tight when I drilled her with my finger last night. Even though she's plenty wet, I spit on my hand and rub my saliva over my sheathed cock.

"Are you okay?" I ask in a low voice, even though I haven't penetrated her yet.

"Do it."

That's my girl. She never was one to mince words. I apply more pressure, nudging at her entrance with more insistence.

She pushes back, arcing her pretty ass up and presenting herself for me.

"That's it, sugar." I decide it's better to go in fast—rip the bandaid off, as they say. I grip her hips and push in. I sense a little resistance give away. She cries out. I reach around the front of her to stroke her clit and move inside her. Just a little —a half inch back, a half inch in. Just to bring her some of the pleasure to counteract the pain. I caress her back, squeeze her ass.

"I'm okay," she gasps after a moment. "It's good."

I pump a little more, going slowly and gently, giving her time to get used to my length. I continue circling her clit lightly with the pad of my finger.

She hums her pleasure and brings her fingers between her legs, pressing over mine.

"You need it there?" I ask, rubbing more firmly. At the same time, I accidentally shove in deeper, a shot of lust rolling through me.

"Oh!" she cries out. "Yes."

"Yes, here?" I rub her clit, "or yes, harder?" I thrust in with more force.

"Harder," she murmurs.

Oh, damn. I don't want to make her regret that, but my control is already slipping. She's so damn tight. So hot.

And all mine.

I still can't get over that part. Each time it dawns on me anew, I want to do every measure of dirty things to her.

I grip her hips with both hands and take a few even strokes. Then I start to bump her ass with my loins, slapping our flesh together, sending my balls against her clit.

"Yes!" she gasps.

"Spread your knees wider," I order.

When she does, it changes the angle, so I can get even deeper inside her. I groan. "You feel so good, Sasha."

"More," she chants. "Harder."

The room starts to spin. Heat spikes the base of my spine. I lean over her torso, propping on one hand to get in deeper, with more force. I fuck her harder. Faster. My breath turns to ragged panting, or maybe that's hers. My thighs start to tremble with the need to release.

She hasn't come yet, so I try to hold back. I rub her clit fast with my free hand.

"Harder!" she commands.

My control unravels. A dark chuckle bursts out of my mouth as I forego her pleasure and just ride in for my own finish. I mold my body to hers, humping that gorgeous ass and plowing deep, deep, deeper still until lights dance before my eyes and come like a fucking speed train.

When I recover I find her red hair bunched in my fist, my mouth on her neck.

A little horrified, I flip her over to her back.

~

SASHA

I THOUGHT GIVING a man a blowjob made me feel powerful, but I had no idea how incredible it felt to see him come undone while inside me.

No wonder sex is power for women. No wonder this is the weapon we wield the best. Because Maxim turned into an animal right before he came. That cool, manicured persona all but disappeared, and he was nothing but raw masculine desire.

Now, as he stares down at me, there's concern etched in his face. He knows he lost control—pulled my hair and fucked me so hard I won't walk straight. He's worried for me, I can tell.

I smile, remembering his words. *You think I could deny you anything after that life-altering blowjob you just gave me?* What about now? Now that he's come inside me? Well, inside a condom, but still inside me. He quickly disposes of the rubber without taking his eyes from my face.

Returning my smile tentatively, he drops kisses between my breasts. He sucks one nipple into his mouth as he massages the other breast. "I'm sorry you didn't come, sugar. I'll make it up to you now."

He's sweet.

I like him sweet. I don't want to like it. I want to resist his charm. Because I've fallen for this man before, and he crushed me.

"I still liked it," I admit. "I didn't come because… "

He lifts his head to meet my eyes.

I sense my face grow warm. I shrug. "It was all new to me. I was fascinated by your orgasm, and then I missed my chance." I don't know why I'm revealing so much again. I guess I'm melting in the warmth of his undivided attention.

His eyes flash dark. "There will be lots of chances. Just give me a few minutes." He sucks my other nipple into his mouth. I wind my fingers through his hair enjoying the riotous sensations he's creating. I didn't come, but I'm not missing the orgasm. It still felt great—both the physical and the chemical rewards. My mood soars along with his. I'm full of that sense of well-being and pleasure. Love, even. Not that I'm in love—no way—but the general feeling of love.

He kisses down my belly and spreads my thighs. I close my eyes as his tongue explores my folds.

"Mmm." Pleasure. I can see how couples stay in bed all day. I now understand how good sex makes people think they're in love.

This is how my mother kept my father ensnared all those years. Although not enough for him to think of her as anything other than an object to serve and please him. An object to pass on.

Maxim finds my clit with his lips and manages to suction them over it. At the same time, he sinks two fingers inside me and starts stroking my inner walls.

"*Gospodi!*" I cry out, arching on the bed. The sensations are so intense. So erotic. I claw at the bedcovers when he doesn't give me a break. He just keeps sucking, keeps stroking.

"Maxim!" My legs thrash beneath me.

He pumps the fingers, bumping my inner wall with the tips every time.

I shriek and pull his hair, frantic, and then I come—a short and fast explosion.

Maxim lifts his mouth away and rubs my clit with this thumb instead.

My eyes roll back in my head. Another short but powerful orgasm rocks through me, and my legs jerk again. Then one more aftershock.

My stomach growls and Maxim chuckles. "Time for breakfast, beautiful." He climbs off me. "But let's get cleaned up first. Come here." He takes my hand and tugs me to the bathroom and in the shower, where he treats me like a queen, lathering me from head to toe, kissing and nuzzling me all over.

I soap his cock, which gets instantly hard again, and then he nails me against the tile and fucks me roughly, pulling out to come on my belly. By the time we both emerge, my legs don't work, and I'm not sure I remember how to speak.

Maxim's phone rings, and he strides out of the bathroom, beautifully naked, gloriously tattooed.

"*Da*." He answers in Russian. "Who did it?" Then, "*Blyat*." He ends the call and looks at me through the bathroom doorway. "Vladimir is dead. The Moscow bratva is in chaos. You need to locate your mother."

CHAPTER 12

 asha

THE CURTNESS in Maxim's voice makes my pulse scurry.

My mother.

"What do you mean? Is she missing?"

Maxim nods as he quickly pulls on his clothing. "Yes."

I grab my clothes and also get dressed. "Do you think she's been killed?"

Maxim hesitates, making my adrenaline kick in, but then he shakes his head. "No. If whoever killed Vladimir wanted her dead, they would have taken care of her at the same time. She's worth something alive if they're interested in your money."

My money.

My heart pounds faster. But that would mean killing me first.

It's the first time since my father's death—actually, the first time ever—I've felt real scared-for-my-life fear. Maxim was trying to warn me about this, but I've lived my whole life as bratva royalty with security guards breathing down my neck. The threat of real danger never sank in before.

My fingers tremble as I dial my mom's number.

I haven't spoken or communicated with her since I left. It's only been a few days, but it strikes me that I should've checked in with her. She just lost my father, after all. I was too busy feeling pissed off and sorry for myself and my situation, I didn't have any brain space left for her. I'm a spoiled, shitty daughter.

My mother picks up with a suspicious tone of voice. With an even deeper stab of guilt, I realize she didn't even have my new U.S. phone number.

"Mama," I gasp in Russian. "Are you all right?"

"Tell her to come to Chicago where I can protect her." Maxim's expression is dark and serious. "Give her your credit card number." The urgency in his voice makes my heartbeat ratchet up another notch. Like he's afraid something will happen to her.

I step into the bathroom for some privacy, not that I'm trying to keep anything from Maxim. I just want to be able to focus on my mother.

"Sasha, you heard the news?"

"Yes, are you safe?"

"I am safe, yes. I am with Viktor."

Viktor, her longtime bodyguard. The one I'd only just realized had feelings for my mother. Thank God. He'll protect her.

"Where are you?"

"I can't tell you. Somewhere safe."

"What happened? What's happening? Mama…"

"It's a coup. Viktor got me out of there before it

happened. There's a power struggle now to see who will rise to the top."

"Maxim says you should come out here where he can protect you. I can put the ticket on my credit card."

"He would say that," my mother says drily.

The hairs on my arms stand up. My fingers go cold. I lower my voice. "What do you mean?"

"Think about it, Sasha. Do you remember your father's will?"

"Yes." Vaguely. I remember that my money wasn't really my money because it went to Maxim. And my mom's money went to Vladimir.

"Who gets the oil well if you die?"

I try to remember the conversation at my father's deathbed. "Vladimir?"

"Yes. But if he's dead, it goes to me. So of course your husband wants us both under his wing. We're the meal tickets."

Queasiness runs through me and my knees go weak. "He wants to protect you," I insist. But I'm suddenly not so sure. How well do I really know Maxim?

Not at all.

"Viktor will protect me. And my staying hidden ensures your safety, too. With Vladimir gone, the pathways to owning that oil well have shortened. We can't make it easy or obvious for anyone to try to seize it. Understand, my dearest?"

"Yes." I'm cold all over.

"Good. Is this your new phone number?"

"Yes."

"I'll be in touch—from a new phone. Be careful, my darling. Play nice with that husband of yours. Make him fall in love—it may keep you alive."

My eyes prick with tears. Does my life really mean so little?

Maxim doesn't want to kill me.

I open the door to the bathroom and find him standing at the window, texting. He doesn't appear to be eavesdropping.

I'm shaky all over, searching his face for some kind of sign. Does my husband want me dead? Is he biding his time in order to find my mother and then planning to kill us both?

A shiver runs down my spine.

No. My mother's just paranoid because Vladimir got killed. It doesn't mean people want to kill the two of us, too.

"She's all right?"

I nod, my head wobbling a bit on my neck. "Yes."

"Is she coming here?"

"No. She says she's safe."

"Does she have protection?"

"Yes." I'm terrified to say anything more.

Maxim nods. "Good. Does she need money?"

"I don't think so."

I wait, but that's the end of it. He doesn't press me or try to convince me to get my mom out here. It sounds like he would've sent her money if she needed it.

He walks toward me and beckons. "Come here, sugar." I don't move, but he folds me into his arms anyway. "You're safe here. No one would try to touch you on Ravil's turf. We would fucking destroy them. I promise you're safe."

They could be lies. I'm not dumb enough to swallow everything he feeds me. In fact, I'll be dissecting every word now. But it still feels good to be held by him. His warmth heats my chilled limbs. His strength makes me feel safe.

I tip my face up. "Who called you?" I hate being suspicious, but I'd be stupid not to ask as many questions as I can think of.

"Ravil."

"Does he know who killed Vladimir?"

"No, but it was poison, which is… strange."

"Why?"

"It's cowardly. Someone making a grab for power should make a powerful move. Shoot him between the eyes, you know?"

A fresh chill washes over me. "What if they're not making a grab for power?" My voice sounds tremulous.

"No one can touch you, Sasha," he says immediately, correctly guessing at my thoughts. "But we should get back to Chicago where I have backup. Okay?"

I nod.

"I'm sorry." He does genuinely sound remorseful. "I know you wanted to stay. I'd just rather play it safe while things are in turmoil. Until we see how things land in Moscow and Dima has his tracking in place to alert us of anyone coming into the country." He searches my face. "Do you want to grab brunch with your friends before we go? Or take a walk on the beach?"

I don't mean to be so transparent, but I jump back into his embrace to hug him, relieved. A man intent on killing his wife would not worry about taking her to the beach first. Or brunch.

He lets out a surprised chuckle. I know the hug is out of character. I've been playing stand-offish since the day we wed. But whatever. The kinky bastard deserves it.

His hand slips under my hair to cup my nape, and he nudges my face up. The kiss he gives me seems meaningful. Important. It's not teasing, not claiming. Firm, but not rough. Like we've reached a different level in our relationship.

When he breaks it, he asks, "Beach or brunch?"

Me being me, I bat my lashes and push my luck. "Both?"

His smirk is both knowing and indulgent. "Okay, sugar. But we *will* be on a plane back to Chicago by nightfall."

"Let's go," I chirp, happy that it's true. He *would* give me anything after good sex.

My mother's right. It would probably even keep him from killing me, if that was his plan.

But I can't believe it is.

My mother is just being paranoid.

And my father trusted him. That hits me for the first time. Maxim's been saying it from the start—that my father picked him because he could protect me best.

I didn't believe it. I thought he chose Maxim to humiliate and punish me. But now that the danger's pressed in close, my view's shifting. Maybe my father foresaw murder, power plays and chaos ensuing after his death. Sending me out of the country *was* smart.

So long as he didn't send me into the arms of a killer.

But he wouldn't knowingly do that. And despite having sent Maxim away, he still trusted him. And Maxim still respected his *pakhan* enough to accept his dying request. Either that, or he just wanted my money.

If only I knew for sure…

～

Maxim

ONLY KAYLA CAN MEET us for brunch, but she seemed like Sasha's closest friend, anyway. We meet her at a beachfront cafe in Santa Monica. I'm itchy with all the people around, but I have a piece tucked in the back of my waistband, with

120

my shirt untucked to cover it. I still don't expect trouble—not yet, anyway—but you never know.

There's something off about Vladimir's death. The fact that the killer didn't just outright announce himself and say he was taking over seems strange to me. I need to know what's going on there to stay on top of any threat that may come Sasha's way.

Kayla shows up still as cute and chipper as she was last night. She throws her arms around Sasha and then me like we're old friends. I kiss her cheek and hold both their chairs like the perfect gentleman.

"Oh my God, I may have just found an agent," Kayla gushes the moment we sit down. "She specializes in commercials, but whatever. I'll start anywhere."

Sasha grabs her hand across the table. "OMG, tell me everything. How did you find her? What's the deal?"

I half-listen as the women dive deep into the story of a chance meeting at her hairdressers that netted a callback this morning.

We're interrupted by the waitress, and we order food. I ask for Mimosas with their best champagne and the women light up.

"So if this works out, I'll have you to thank, really." Kayla beams at Sasha after the waitress leaves.

"How is that?" I ask.

Kayla turns her wide blue eyes on me. She's got that *Buffy the Vampire Slayer* look going—a cute little dynamo in the All-American way. "Sasha's the one who got me going to Monique, our hairdresser. She's way out of my budget, but Sasha sniffed out the best in L.A., and that studio is where things happen. I mean, I felt like Monique practically acted as my agent with the agent. You know? Like she made the introduction while we were both sitting next to each other with foils in our hair."

Sasha shifts in her chair and looks at her manicure. "Well, I'm happy for you, but also—I'm so jealous, bitch."

Something twists in my chest. Sasha had dreams. Maybe I hoped she hadn't—that her theatre degree was just some fluffy thing to do while she enjoyed college. Sasha could probably buy that agent's agency, she could fund her own movies, but I doubted that would be as exciting as the achievement of the Hollywood dream. Getting discovered. Auditioning. Nailing the part. Making it big. Those experiences couldn't be bought.

But no problem can't be fixed. That's my motto, and it's never failed me. So I'll have to figure something out. Something that lights my bride up back in Chicago.

Our drinks arrive, and I lift my champagne flute in Kayla's direction. "To new opportunities."

"For all of us," Kayla counters, and we clink glasses.

Sasha steals a look at me. She's been doing that since we checked out of the hotel, and I hired a driver for the day. He's sitting in his car somewhere nearby with our belongings safely stowed.

I reach for her hand under the table and squeeze it, and she meets my gaze with a surprisingly vulnerable look. Like part of her wants to slam the door in my face, and the other part wants everything from me—more than she believes I'll give.

It unsettles me. Not because I wouldn't give her everything she needed. I mean, I hadn't thought about it, but I probably would. I'm unnerved because I recognize that chaotic sense of falling. It mirrors my own.

I hadn't felt it with her until this moment because falling wasn't in question. She was an obligation. A duty. A job. I didn't make myself vulnerable when I married her. I made myself rich. My heart was never in play.

But after cracking her shell—after things got real—it's impossible not to care about her. She gave herself to me today. Not just the sex. I don't believe a woman's virginity is some huge momentous gift. I don't think it's something Sasha should've been required to save for her husband. But the fact is, she did. And I had the privilege of taking it.

"Look at you two, making googly eyes at each other," Kayla says.

Sasha pulls her hand from mine and picks up her champagne flute. "Yeah, he might not be that bad, as far as husbands go." She says it lightly, and Kayla laughs but something kindles inside me.

I wink at her. Maybe we'll become more than an arranged marriage.

Kayla points at me and makes her face stern. "You'd better be good to her," she warns.

My lips twist with amusement. "Or?"

"Or I'll kick your ass."

I nod and cross my heart with my finger. "She's safe with me. I promise."

Sasha

Maxim is damn sweet with Kayla. I haven't had a boyfriend before, but Kayla, Sheri, and Ashley have, and I know from experience that a guy hanging around patiently for girl talk is unusual.

Maxim's on his best behavior, though, charming Kayla

without being flirty. Treating brunch like a continuation of last night's party, with the champagne and orange juice. He lets us linger for two hours before he finally tosses cash on the table and stands.

I'm certain he's going to say we have to go straight to the airport, but after we say goodbye to Kayla, he laces fingers with me. "Want to walk on the beach?"

I swallow and nod, stealing a glance at his handsome face.

Gospodi, I do not want to fall in love with this man.

I can't be crushed again. And worse—he may want me dead although I don't think so.

"Boardwalk or sand?"

"Sand," I breathe. Living near the beach was one of the best parts of living in L.A. The weather, the ocean, the culture are all so different from Moscow. When I was here, I pretended I was something else. A native Californian, consumed only with my looks, my health and acting.

We walk down to the sand and take our shoes off. Maxim cuffs his slacks. His shirt sleeves are already rolled up his forearms, giving everyone at brunch a view of his heavily corded forearms and the colorless tattoos that crawl up them.

Maxim takes both pairs of our shoes in one hand and with his other intertwines his fingers with mine. The beach is noisy, teeming with perfect bodies and families with children.

"I loved living here," I admit out loud. I don't know why I'm sharing. Why I think Maxim would even care.

He glances down at me. "I can tell."

My breath catches at those simple words. Like he's been paying attention. What if he did actually care? Or come to care? The thought of it makes my heart race, and my hands grow clammy, like I'm still a teenager.

"I wish I'd come to visit you then."

I look up. The wind ruffles his sandy hair. He fits in here with his broad shoulders and well-kept body. The expensive button-down shirt open at the collar. He just needs a tan and for his hair to pick up some highlights to look like Californian royalty. "Really? Why?"

One corner of his lips lifts for a moment then quickly fades. "I'll bet you were something to see."

I hip-bump him, interrupting our casual pace when he has to side step to recover. "What does that mean?" I demand with a laugh. I'm fishing now—I can't help it. I've always been starved for attention, and here, I'm finally getting some.

"I liked seeing you with your friends." He lifts our joined hands to his lips and kisses my fingers. "I got to see the real you."

I'm embarrassed at how clammy my hand gets. How hard my pathetic heart starts pounding.

"I don't even know the real me," I find myself saying. It's the truth although I don't know where it came from.

"That was the real you," Maxim says, like he knows for sure. Like he's seen into my broken soul that quickly. That easily.

"What was?"

"Fun. Lively. The life of the party. But also generous. You're a good friend—I can tell. You guys support each other. You want the best for each other."

I think of my jealousy over Kayla's career and feel a pang of guilt.

As if Maxim reads my mind, he says, "You wish you were still here. Living with them."

The words are unexpected, and they bring up buried emotion. My eyes get hot and wet. I blink rapidly, tossing my hair in the breeze and pretending a little sand got in them. "Staying here was never an option." My voice only chokes a little. "I knew I was on borrowed time the entire four years I was here. I was lucky Igor let me come at all."

"He loved you," Maxim says simply.

This time the unexpected hot tears come as a flood. Two streak down my face before I can catch them. "*Gospodi,*" I mutter, swiping at them with the back of my free hand. "I don't know about that."

"He did. He was a shitty father in many ways, but you were his only child, and he did love you very much."

"His form of love sucked, then," I say bitterly, but guilt fills my chest. It's not entirely true. I have memories of him swooping me up into his arms as a little girl. Tossing me into the air. Making me laugh. Bringing over presents and sweets. I used to look forward to his visits like he was freaking Santa Claus. But that's fucked up. He should have been my dad, not some magical godfather who showed up when he wanted and bought my love. I lived for his attention because I didn't have it often enough.

Maxim shrugs. "I'm sure it could've been better. Could've been worse, too. He was who he was. My mother was a lying cunt who tricked me into waiting for her for years. She should've done better, but she didn't. Igor gave me more in comparison. So he had my loyalty."

I'm awash in cold at Maxim's words. Honored that he shared this sliver of his true self with me. His broken self. I knew there had to be a story about why he served my father so loyally. Everyone seemed to have one.

"Your mother tricked you?" I ask softly.

Maxim looks past me to the ocean as he takes easy steps, our feet sinking into the softer sand. "When she brought me to the orphanage, she told me she'd be back. To be good. And so I waited. I waited for years. Until I finally got smart enough to figure out she'd suckered me. Ruined by women's lies seems to be a theme with me." He throws me a meaningful glance, and my insides tumble. My body goes hot and cold wishing I'd never ruined his life the way I did.

"I'm sorry—"

"Don't." He cuts me off with the harsh syllable. Like he just showed me too much and regrets it.

I don't dare speak even though my breath hangs in my chest, suspended. Needing to come out in a rush.

After an excruciating moment, Maxim saves me by going on. "I ran away from the orphanage at fourteen and tried to make it on my own. I did all right. Learned to pickpocket and slept in an empty building I broke into.

"Igor saw me on the streets. He had a habit of recruiting down-on-their-luck boys from the street. The bratva headquarters had warm beds and food. Plenty of cash to go around if we proved ourselves. Every member needed an errand boy. Hell, they loved training us up in their own images. Violent and ruthless but with rules."

"Were you my father's errand boy?"

Maxim nods. "I learned from the best." His smile is sad, like he doesn't love the man he was. Or perhaps still is. "I paid attention. I listened and watched. Igor figured out I was smart when I started fixing the problems some of the other brigadiers got into. That's how I got my title as fixer. I was too young for leadership, so he kept me by his side as strategist. Sent me out when problems arose to fix them."

"You're grateful to him."

Maxim nods. "I will forever be grateful. The life he gave me was so much better than the one I had. I was nothing, and he made me into a powerful man."

"And I ruined that."

"No." Maxim stops and looks out at the ocean. "I thought so at the time—but no." He turns to look at me, and it takes all my courage not to flinch away. "You did me a favor. My life is ten times better here than it was in Russia. Ravil has Chicago at his feet, and he shares the wealth generously. I'm happy here."

I work to swallow, but I can't. I want to ask if he forgives me, but the words get clogged in my throat.

"Did you know? That he knew it wasn't true?"

"No." Maxim removes his hand from mine, and I register the loss for a second until I realize it was to brush my hair out of my face. My belly flutters when his knuckles make the whisper contact. "But I wondered. It explains why I'm alive. I figured he wasn't sure, and that's why he hedged by sending me out of the country." He loops a hand around my throat, his thumb lightly stroking the column of my neck. "But he knew for sure. Which I guess is proof of his love for you."

I scrunch up my forehead. "How, exactly?"

"He didn't call your bullshit. He respected you enough to get rid of me since you wanted me gone. And I may be mistaken, but I believe he was pretty fucking fond of me. I was his protégé. Made in his image and all that."

My face flushes. I'd wanted to hurt him, but I hadn't actually wanted him gone. My father had kept me away from people and business most of the time, but when he took us on vacation the next year and Maxim wasn't there, I'd felt the loss acutely.

"I-I was stupid and spiteful. If he'd killed you, I never would have forgiven myself."

Maxim brushes my lower lip with the pad of his thumb. "Igor probably knew that, too."

"I think you give him more credit than he deserves."

Maxim shakes his head. "No. I learned at his side. He considered every angle before he made a move. He must've decided removing me was the best solution for both of us.

Same as he decided unifying us now would complete the circle."

Something huge rocks inside me. I'm not sure I buy that Maxim and I were meant to be married. That our marriage is closure or a completion. I still suspect it was my father punishing me. But hearing the other possibility blows open the roof on my current thinking. Those thoughts are dangerous, though.

Especially after my conversation with my mother.

Maxim touches my nose seeming to read my mind with that uncanny ability of his. "Or maybe it's all his sick sense of humor. He's cackling from the grave right now at both of us."

I put my hands on my hips. "I fail to see how this situation is so awful for you."

The shoes drop to the sand, and he loops an arm around my waist and yanks me up to him.

"No, you're right," he murmurs, bringing his lips right above mine. "At the moment, it doesn't seem so bad for me." He brushes his lips over mine. My breasts press against his ribs, and I stroke a hand under his shirt to feel those rock hard abs I saw earlier. "I have a hot, rich wife." He squeezes my ass, pulling my hips up against him. "And she may be a handful, but punishing her is quite possibly the highlight of my life."

The highlight of his life.

He can't mean that.

I mean… of course, he doesn't. That's ridiculous.

"The highlight of your sex life?"

Maxim smirks. "Definitely." He nips my lower lip.

I kiss him, my hand stroking under his shirt to his back. When I find the gun concealed there, I flinch and retract my hand.

Maxim cradles the back of my head and angles my face

up for a real kiss. His tongue sweeps between my lips, and he pulls on them, repositions, kisses me again. My nipples get hard beneath my bra, and I lose my breath.

Despite how sore I am down there, I find myself craving more sex. I want to feel everything. All the positions, all the orgasms. The threats Maxim made about implements and bondage.

"Too bad we checked out already," I breathe when he breaks the kiss.

His eyes are dark. "*Da.* But I already wore you out, no?" His smile is wicked. He stoops to pick up our shoes. "I'll have to take you home for our next round." He winks. "You have the whole plane ride to recover."

I gently push him away. "You're pretty sure of yourself."

He takes my hand and changes direction, walking back down the beach the way we came. "Oh, I have no doubt you'll keep me working, *caxapok.* Docile isn't in your nature, is it?"

I smile, irrationally happy that he seems to be celebrating the very thing my father couldn't stand about me. "Nope," I confirm.

"It's all right. I can handle you." The words are slightly offensive, but the warmth behind them keeps me floating.

The real question is—can I handle him?

And my most gnawing fear is that I can't.

That I'm in way, way over my head with this man.

With my husband.

CHAPTER 13

 *axim*

I GET us on an afternoon flight to Chicago, and it's evening by the time we get out of the cab back to the Kremlin. I'm downright chipper—so far from the mood I was in when I got on the plane yesterday to chase down my runaway bride.

I'm not foolish enough to believe her conquered, but she's certainly getting tamer. Or maybe I'm fool enough to believe that just because I finally got my dick wet. I do know sex can turn men into idiots—Ravil is the prime example of that when he kidnapped his pregnant one night stand.

We take the elevator to the penthouse where we find Oleg walking out the door, smelling of Nikolai's cologne.

"What's this?" I ask. "Going to hear your girl play?"

Oleg gives a barely perceptible nod. Communicating with him is more a game of mind-reading than anything else.

"What girl? Play where?" Sasha touches Oleg's meaty arm. "Oleg, you have a girlfriend?"

131

It's an innocent touch, but some primitive part of me bristles at seeing her fingers on another man's skin.

I catch her wrist to pull it away from Oleg and twist her arm behind her back. "What did I tell you?" I murmur in her ear. "No touching other men, *caxapok*. You wouldn't want me to throat-punch Oleg—I think we all know I'm the guy who'd lose that fight."

Sasha's laugh is throaty. She squirms against my hold, but it's only for show. She likes to be restrained, I can tell.

My dick gets chubby thinking of all the dirty things I want to do to her.

Oleg eyes us both doubtfully. Wariness is his usual state of being, even with us, his suitemates and bratva brothers.

I fill Sasha in. "Oleg goes to hear a local band every week. He's sweet on the singer."

My party girl lights up, turning those shining blue eyes on me. "Can we go?" She shifts her questioning gaze to Oleg then back at me.

My plans were definitely more like locking her in my bedroom again and never letting her out, but it's impossible to refuse her after she showed me her sweet side. Ravishing my new bride again will have to wait.

I look at Oleg. "Is that all right with you?" Oleg ranks below me, but he's our enforcer and can literally crush a man with his bare hands. I'm not about to fuck with him when a woman's involved.

He stares at us for a moment then shrugs his muscled shoulders.

"Okay. We'll meet you there. Rue's Lounge?"

Oleg nods.

"Is it okay if we bring the whole gang?"

Oleg walks away.

Well, it wasn't a *no*.

I wink at Sasha and flash my key card at our penthouse door.

"Our princess has been found!" Dima exclaims from his computer station in the living room. His twin sits on the couch with Pavel watching *The Boys*.

"Yes. Did you locate that shock collar to keep her from straying again?" I tease.

Sasha whirls on me to make sure I'm kidding, and I grin.

"*Mudak.*" She smacks me with the back of her hand. "You guys want to go see Oleg's girlfriend play?"

I like that Sasha's already playing social coordinator with my brothers. She's not the shy violet waiting for me to take the lead. When she's in a room, she owns it. I love it about her, but I have a feeling it will also cost me dearly at times.

Like every time she innocently touches another man.

"Yeah, I'll go." Dima answers first.

Pavel turns off the television. "Sure." He gets up and Nikolai follows.

"What about Ravil and Lucy?" I ask.

"I think they're occupied." Nikolai waggles his brows, and the rest of us groan.

"Yeah…" I look at Sasha, wondering again why I agreed to this when I could have her naked in my bed by now.

"Give me twenty minutes," she says, zipping off to my—our—bedroom suite."

I glance at the guys before I follow. "Make it thirty-five."

I catch Sasha in the closet where I tear her dress off her body. "Oh! *Gospodi*, Maxim." She whirls to face me, her hands against my chest, her eyes wide with surprise.

It's easy to forget she's innocent, but I see it glimmer through her bravado now. There's a touch of astonishment and nerves along with the excitement.

I trail my hand up her ass, my middle finger tracing along

her g-string into her crack. I nuzzle her neck. "I want you again, *lyubimaya*. Are you too sore?"

Rather than answer, she drops to her knees and unbuttons my pants.

Fuck. I'm an asshole because I know that means she's too sore, but I'm incapable of stopping that lush mouth from wrapping around my dick again. She pulls out my cock and fists it at the base, taking me deep into her mouth.

I tighten my fingers in her hair then force them to open and massage the back of her head instead. "Twice in one day. You make me feel like a fucking king." My voice sounds two octaves deeper than usual.

Sasha's blue gaze comes up to meet mine. She knows she's a badass at giving head—I can tell by the blaze of glory in her eyes.

I gather her hair into a ponytail in the back to get the full view of her face. "So sweet... so fucking good." My head drops back. I'm babbling now, surrendering to the delicious sensations of her tongue swirling beneath my cock, her cheeks hollowing out to suck me hard. "I won't last long, *lyubimaya*." I don't know when she became *my love*. One minute she was a pain in my ass, now she's becoming my whole world.

My thighs start to shake. I can't help myself, I start to direct, pulling her mouth over me faster, thrusting into her throat. I close my eyes, letting the pressure build, the pleasure intensifying.

"Fuck, Sasha," I curse. "I'm going to come."

Like last time, she doesn't pull off, instead sucks harder and faster. I shout and come and she takes it, swallowing it all down before she comes off with a saucy smile.

I zip and pull her up to kiss hard, walking her backward

until her ass hits the wall. "You want my mouth on you now, sugar?"

I see hunger and need on her face, but she shakes her head. "Rain check."

I nuzzle her neck and slip my hand into one of her bra cups. "I'm sorry if I was too rough with you this morning."

"You were perfect," she murmurs.

I tip her chin up to kiss her again. I want to consume her. Own her so fully she never runs from me. Make her fall in love.

Damn. That's it, isn't it? I want my wife to fall in love with me.

How in the fuck did that happen? When did that happen?

"Come on, I don't want to miss Oleg's girlfriend play." Sasha pushes gently at my chest. I steal one more kiss before I release her.

"Sing," I correct because the woman he likes is the singer in the band. "She's not his girlfriend. Just a girl he likes. Maybe you can help him get her number. He seemed like he was going to bash my face in the last time when I tried to talk to her on his behalf."

"Ooh, this is going to be fun." Sasha digs through her suitcases, pulling out a pair of skinny jeans and a hot bustier. A pair of high heels completes the outfit.

I change my shirt and watch her flit about the room and bathroom getting ready. I don't know why I'm so fascinated by every move she makes. Her quick application of make up. The brushing of her thick hair. Rolling a scent on her wrists and throat. I catch her wrist and bring it to my nose. It's nothing cloying—not some chemical perfume smell that will make me want to shower after she hugs me. It's a warm citrus scent that makes me want to eat her up.

"Ready?"

"I was born ready." She tosses that saucy grin at me, and I scoop my forearm under her ass, scooping her up to straddle me. She shrieks as I carry her out the bedroom door and into the suite where Dima, Nikolai and Pavel wait.

Dima flicks a brow. "I won."

"Won what?" I ease Sasha down to her feet and loop an arm around her waist.

"The bet. They didn't think you'd, um, convince Sasha to stay in less time than it took Ravil to keep Lucy from running."

"I will throat punch all of you," I warn, tugging Sasha past the assholes and out the door. "Ignore them," I tell her. "We both know I've won nothing yet."

CHAPTER 14

S asha

    Rue's Lounge is a hipster lounge—grungy but very cool. It's located in the basement of a more industrial area of town. The band hasn't started, but Oleg has staked out the closest two-top to the stage where he sits with a pint of craft beer in front of him.

"Hey, how's it going?" I touch his shoulder before remembering with a smile that Maxim doesn't like it.

I'm irrationally pleased by his irrational possessiveness. Especially because he doesn't make me feel like a whore, he makes me feel desirable. *Highly* desirable.

I take the free chair next to Oleg while Maxim and the other three guys scrounge chairs from other tables and arrange them around our tiny table. A cocktail waitress arrives promptly, and we all get a round of the local brew on tap. As we sit, the place starts filling up.

I lean forward, thoroughly enjoying myself. Unlike my father's men—these guys are friendly. I'm their roommate's wife not the boss' daughter. It's a different vibe here entirely. They seem to have a sense of humor and casual

RENEE ROSE

affection with each other, like we're all in the sitcom *Friends* or something. "So what is the story with Lucy and Ravil?"

Nikolai and Pavel groan and sit back in their chairs. Oleg barely takes his eyes off the empty stage. Like a dog waiting at the door for its owner to show, even though the car hasn't pulled into the garage yet. Dima looks at Maxim to tell the story.

"Ravil hooked up with Lucy at this one-night-stand kind of thing last Valentine's Day. It happened at this BDSM club in Washington, D.C. and was anonymous—no names, no phone numbers exchanged. Flash forward to this month— Ravil goes to hire some big shot defense attorney for one of our guys. When he shows up at her office, he finds Lucy, pregnant with his child."

I clap my hand over my mouth. "No!" I also want to hear so much more about the BDSM club, but I don't want to stop the story.

"So Ravil loses his shit. He's usually level-headed as fuck. I mean, as the cell Fixer, I almost never have to fix." Maxim spreads his hands. "More than half the operation is legit. Force is only employed when necessary."

"So what happened?" I'm impatient for the love story. It sounds better than fiction.

Maxim shrugs. "So he kidnaps her."

"What?"

"Yeah. He was deeply offended that she hadn't told him. Took it really personally. He moves her into his suite and puts Oleg on her door, so she can't leave. Tells her she has to work remotely until the baby's born."

I shake my head slowly. "That's not right." I suddenly don't like Ravil much.

"No kidding. And it's my job to make sure shit like this

138

doesn't blow up in our faces, right? So I looked at it from all angles, and all I came up with was one fix."

I raise my brows. "What was it?"

"Make her fall in love. It was clear he already had it for her badly. Otherwise, he wouldn't have been hurt. So that was my only fix. Love."

I sit back in my chair relieved for Lucy. More than a little impressed with Maxim.

Was that his solution for us, too? I want to ask, but my pride won't let me.

"And it worked," I finish for him.

"Almost didn't. But yeah. Thank fuck."

The band comes out, and I watch Oleg's body react. He doesn't move, but I see his muscles stiffen, the intensity of his gaze on the only female in the band almost frightening.

She's punk-goth-beautiful. Like a modern-day Blondie, she has a platinum bob with bangs and thick black eyeliner. Her nose is pierced, and she has perfect bone structure—one of those heart-shaped faces that will make her model-beautiful well into old age. She's wearing a micro skirt with fishnets and Doc Martens underneath. Her top is early Madonna midriff style with a torn-out neckline to make it hang open over one shoulder. She's rocking the bad-girl rock and roll thing, and I sort of instantly love her.

I mean, if Oleg wasn't obsessed, I probably wouldn't have looked twice. She's nothing like me or my kind of friends. But his obsession makes me curious. She picks up the mic.

The place has filled since we arrived—a din of laughing and talking now makes it necessary to raise our voices to be heard. The crowd fits with the band—a little grunge-punk—and people seem to know each other. Like Oleg isn't the only guy who comes to hear the band on the regular.

"Hey everyone, thanks for coming out," she says. "I'm Story, and we are the Storytellers."

Even though she's talking into the mic, people don't stop to listen. But that's how it is at a bar or lounge. It's not a concert where the musicians get the audience's undivided attention. They're background here.

Oleg's thick brows go down like he wants to smash some skulls over it.

He elbows Nikolai and puts his fingers in a ring to his lips. Nikolai mimics the gesture and gives a loud whistle that gets people's attention.

"Hey, thanks," Story says, smiling our way. Her gaze bounces and returns to Oleg, and she seems to give him a special, secret smile. "And thank you to Rue for having us out again, tonight. This is our favorite place to play." She waves, and a woman with heavy piercings and a blue mohawk behind the bar waves back.

"First song we're going to sing is called 'Let's Go.'" The band launches into a well-rehearsed upbeat song. Story's lyrics are clever. The musical hooks are perfect. I don't know that much about the music industry, but I'm surprised these guys haven't gone beyond Chicago. They're great.

We sit and watch. I don't dare attempt more conversation with Oleg sitting at the table. He clearly is here for the band, and I don't want to be rude. Instead I watch the band, Oleg, the other guys at our table. Maxim watches me.

I lean over and kiss his jaw. "This is fun."

He drags me out of my chair and onto his lap. "*You're* fun." I settle into his embrace. It feels easy and natural and, simultaneously, thrilling.

The next song is slower, and Story walks out to the edge of the stage to sing. Like me, she's comfortable with attention. This isn't just about the music, it's about the interaction with the audience. She works to make connections—looking people in the eyes when she sings, making her face expressive to go with the words.

I can see how Oleg fell in love with this persona. I doubt she has any interest in him, though. It probably just seems that way to him because of the way she performs.

I watch song after song, enjoying the whole scene.

By the end of the second set, they have a drunken crowd packed in and dancing right in the tiny dance area in front of the stage. We're on the side, lucky to have seats right off the dance floor but still beside the stage. The band strikes up what seems to be their big, fun hit. The end-of-the-night finale. The audience cheers, clearly familiar with it. Story prances to the edge of the stage near us, belting out the song. She walks down the steps and joins the dancers on the dance floor.

Oleg's back goes ramrod stiff, his meaty hands closing into fists like he's the bouncer ready to throw out anyone who touches her.

She's touching them, though. They fall in line behind her and tour the lounge, loudly singing along in a crazy conga-line. "Come on." I jump to my feet to join.

Maxim gives me that indulgent smile and slowly unfolds from his chair, guarding my back as I join the hilarity. Story snakes the group around. Instead of heading back on stage, she stands on my empty chair then in the center of our table. The crowd cheers.

She steadies herself with a hand on Oleg's shoulder. The moment she touches him, his hand shoots out to hold her waist. She loops a leg over one of his broad shoulders, straddling it.

The crowd cheers—I think possibly at her audacity of climbing her audience like a jungle gym.

Oleg's elbow bends up to secure her with his hand splayed at her lower back. When he stands slowly, there are more whoops and cheers and some very drunken crowd members start scrambling on each other's shoulders like they're going to have a chicken fight. Oleg carries his queen to the center of the dance floor where her hive swarms around her, glorying in the royal position he put her in.

The band goes on for three encores before Oleg gently deposits her on her feet on stage, and the entire place goes wild with cheering for him, for the band, and especially for Story, their captivating lead singer.

"*Gospodi!*" I shout to Maxim. "Does that always happen?"

Maxim and his roommates share bewildered expressions. "I've never seen it before."

Oleg comes back and sits, his expression impassive, but with a visible flush under his stubble.

The guys offer fists to bump, but he ignores them, folding his arms across his chest to continue watching his obsession. She's out of breath, laughing and thanking the crowd. Promising to be back the same time next week.

Story and the band members bow and wave and then start packing up their own equipment—I guess they're too small to have a sound crew.

The overhead fluorescent lights flash on. "Last call!" Rue shouts from behind the bar.

Maxim orders another round for everyone, pulling me back onto his lap.

When Story comes off the stage, she has a whole crew of people waiting to accost her, but me being me, I stand up and give a little wave like we know each other.

She meets my eye and smiles.

"She's coming!" I tell Oleg.

For one second, I think he's going to bolt. He surges forward to stand, but Dima and Nikolai each clamp a hand on his shoulders and hold him back. "Be cool," Nikolai tells him.

Story comes over. Her smile is curious, like she's not sure if we *do* know each other or what I'm going to say.

"Hey, great show," I tell her, stretching out my hand. "My name is Sasha." She shakes it. "You were phenomenal. I had to come see because I know my friend Oleg thinks the world of you guys." I gesture toward Oleg.

"*Oleg*," she repeats like she's been wanting to know his name. She stretches out her hand to him.

Now he surges up from the table, and this time the twins let him. He clasps her hand in his and doesn't look like he wants to ever let it go.

"We haven't formally met."

"He's mute but not deaf," I explain because she's obviously waiting for him to say something. "He loves your music. We all do," I amend, gesturing to the rest of the guys, who lift their hands in greeting.

"Where are you from?" she asks.

My accent is thicker when I've been drinking. "Russia."

"All of you?" She's looking at Oleg, who still hasn't released her hand.

"Yes."

"Can we buy you a drink?" Maxim asks, standing beside me. When Oleg frowns, Maxim amends, "Oleg's always good for an after-set drink. Anytime."

"I can't tonight but maybe next time." She pulls her hand out of Oleg's grasp. "Thanks for letting me fuck with you tonight. You were a good sport."

"The pleasure was his," Maxim fills in after the awkward pause when she realized he couldn't answer.

After she walks away, Oleg sinks into his chair, glowering at the table.

"You can't kill us because Sasha did it," Maxim says, winking at me. "My brilliant wife."

His brilliant wife.

I warm in the glow of three words I never imagined I'd hear from Maxim's lips. Straddling his lap, I kiss him. This was fun. I feel like I belong, like everything is easy and light —like my college days.

Maybe Maxim was right.

Maybe my father did choose a husband for me who he believed could make me happy.

Nah, that's assigning him too much credit. But at least it seems like his stupid scheme for me wasn't the worst thing that's ever happened.

axim

THE NEXT DAY, Ravil seeks me out when Sasha's in our bedroom.

For all the glory of our penthouse, we don't have any office space. It's why Dima's set up in the living room. Ravil had a desk installed in his suite for Lucy to work from, but his is out in the living room, too. In the past, that worked. We're all in the same business. No one needed privacy to conduct business. Now that we have women living with us, I suspect that will need to change.

There are plenty of office spaces and meeting rooms on the lower floors of the Kremlin, so we could set up a separate business suite.

"Any word from Galina?"

"Sasha spoke to her. She's fine, just lying low. She's with Viktor."

"Viktor who?" Ravil looks suspicious.

I shrug. "He was just a brigadier. I think he played body-guard to Galina and Sasha. Who knows, maybe they were lovers."

"Ah."

"How are things shaking out in Moscow?"

"Leonid Kuznetsov and Ivan Lebedev both are claiming power. Whether they will divvy up Igor's cells or one will kill the other remains to be seen."

"Hmm. My money's on Kuznets, how about you?" I remember the cell *pakhan,* Leonid Kuznetsov. He was smart and ruthless. A little too greedy, a little too proud, but he'd make a decent leader.

"Same, yes. He's asking for our support."

"Did you give it to him?"

"Yes. I'd rather deal with him than Ivan. That man is unreasonable."

"Agreed. So it doesn't seem like Sasha or Galina were part of this coup? Have you heard anything?"

"No one seems to care. Other than the initial call when I heard Galina was missing, no one's mentioned her again. No, I don't think they were part of it."

I exhale a breath I'd been holding since Ravil first called with the news when we were in California. "Thank fuck."

"Yes." Ravil considers me. "She's becoming more willing?"

I remember the image of my beautiful bride on her back this morning, her legs over my shoulders, moaning my name. "We seem to be getting along."

Ravil's lips twitch. "Good. That's better for everyone."

"Tell me about it," I say drily. For a while there, marrying Sasha felt like a prison sentence. I know she felt the same way. "I'm keeping her on constant watch until Dima's worked out some kind of alarm system to let us know if any bratva member enters this country. Even without Sasha in the picture, it will be a good mechanism to have in place."

"Yes. We don't need Ivan sending someone over here to install his own team in our place. I already upped security on the building the moment Vladimir was killed."

I nod, unsurprised. Ravil is a smart man.

"Sasha won't try to run again?"

She might. I'm not dumb enough to think I have her tamed or that she trusts me. We seem to be getting along, but I know firsthand how she can flip on a dime. Still, when she ran, she didn't run far, and she knew I'd follow. In other words, she didn't run in earnest, she was just making me work.

"I can handle her."

The bedroom door opens, and Sasha comes out in her running shorts. "I'm going for a run." She has that haughty air about her that she had when I first brought her back.

"Not alone, you're not."

She ignores me and walks to the door. "Better hurry, then."

Fuck me. I'm already in my running clothes because I anticipated her desire, but I scramble to grab my keycard and wallet. I catch her in the hall outside the penthouse, wrapping an arm around her waist to drag her back to me. "Hey. Hey. What's the deal?"

When she fights me, I nail her up against the wall and pin her wrists beside her head. "*Caxapok*. What happened?" I try to look at her face, but she's looking through me. I drop my face into her neck and nuzzle. "Why are you making me work? What did I do wrong?"

Her breath rasps between us for a moment. "What were you saying about me?" There's accusation in her tone.

Aw, fuck. I rewind, trying to remember what I'd said to Ravil. What she'd heard.

I hold her wrists firmly and pin her with my most direct stare. "I was not being disrespectful, I swear on your father's grave."

She makes a scoffing sound and starts to look away, but her gaze bounces back to mine. She's unsure. I don't know what made her so damn insecure. A half an hour ago, we were in post-coital bliss, her tucked against my side purring. But I get it. Nobody likes to be talked about. It probably perpetuates that feeling that she's not in charge of her own life.

"Ravil asked if you were going to keep running. I said I could handle you. I'm sorry. I did *not* mean to fuck this up. Did I hurt your feelings?"

I press a kiss to her temple, her cheek. Her nose.

"How are you going to handle me?" she asks sullenly. She's sulking, but I can tell whatever barrier she'd thrown up is dropping.

"Hey." I shift in front of her when she looks away. "I'm sorry. I didn't mean anything other than that if you run, I'll chase. You already know that, don't you, *lyubimaya*?"

"Why was he asking?"

I narrow my eyes. "What's this about?"

"Don't gaslight me. I want to know why you two were discussing me."

I release her wrists and straighten, realizing there's something more seriously amiss here. She's genuinely worried about something.

"Ravil's my *pakhan*. We were discussing business. You're part of our business now. If someone comes after you, Ravil's cell—my cell—will be the ones who have to take care of it. That's all."

She swallows and nods, but I'm not certain I convinced her.

"Listen, I know it's hard to trust. This marriage blindsided both of us, and your whole life changed in an instant. I'm sorry about that. But I'm not planning any more surprises. I'm not going to make decisions on your behalf unless it's to protect you. You have my word."

The fight goes out of Sasha, and she leans against the wall like it's holding her up.

"Are we okay?"

She nods, but it looks a little shaky.

"You still want to run?"

Her nod quickens. "Definitely."

I hit the elevator button and gesture toward it when the doors immediately open. "After you, *caxapok*."

SASHA

THE FIST in my solar plexus only loosens part way with Maxim's promises. We step into the elevator together, and I have to breathe down my anxiety.

I hate living with suspicions. I wish mom had never suggested he might be after my money, that he might be trying to kill me because now the slightest thing gets me paranoid.

Not that hearing them talking about me in low voices can be categorized as *the slightest thing*. I think I had good reason to question him.

My mom texted me this morning from a new number to tell me she was still safe but not to contact her. She told me to get a burner phone, warning me that Maxim had access to all my call history, even if I deleted messages.

Of course, I know she's right. I knew he'd put a tracker in my phone the moment he handed it to me.

The trouble is—how do I even get a burner phone when my husband won't let me out of his sight? And even if my mom's wrong—even if I can trust Maxim—is this any way to live?

I can't be suffocated like this for much longer without going nuts. I know Maxim said it was temporary, but I don't know if I can believe that. Or how long temporary will be.

When we get downstairs, I take off running on the route he showed me last time. He paces beside me, honoring my silence, but sending me assessing glances.

I appreciate that he sees me. I'm not trying to hide things from him—if I were, I'd like to think my acting skills would keep him from seeing so damn much. But I have to admit, it feels good to have him paying so much attention.

And caring.

It's hard to believe my mom when I consider how attentive Maxim has been. Then again, if I'm his Golden Goose, he would want to be attentive. He'd want to keep me wrapped around his finger, so I didn't notice how tight the leash was.

I run farther than I should—after a few days off and the late nights drinking, my body is off-schedule, but it feels good. Moves the anxiety out of my pores with my sweat. Clears the knot in my belly with my breath.

We get back and both shower—not together. Maxim seems to realize I'm not in the mood. When he gets out, a towel wrapped around his six-pack, I confront him.

"I want a car."

He's back to playing Mr. Cool—nothing showing in his

expression. He drops the towel and pulls on a pair of boxer briefs. "You want freedom."

I feel seen again. "Yes."

"Do you have a license?"

"Yep. I got one in California when I was a student."

"Okay." He nods. "Let's go buy you a car, then." There's reservation in his tone, like he's making a concession.

"Yeah?"

"Of course. I don't have access to your inheritance yet, but I can cover it. We'll get you something flashy. A convertible? How about a Corvette?"

I'm stunned. I never expected him to agree. Especially not so easily. "Lambo."

"Lamborghini it is." He walks toward me in nothing but his boxer briefs. He sprouts an erection as he gets closer. "You're going to look hot in your Lambo." His lids droop, and he grabs me by the waist and pulls me against his body.

"Mmm." I hum and look up at him. I didn't expect him to agree. It feels like another piece of evidence that he's operating in good faith.

Not trying to kill me.

"But Sasha?"

"Yes?"

"Lambo's are fast." His lips twitch in a smile. "Please don't make me chase you." His hand drops to squeeze my ass. "Promise to be good?"

Lust ripples through me at his insinuation of punishment. I remember how hot my last punishment was. How much I like this game. "I promise," I murmur, only half meaning it.

"Hmm." He doesn't believe me because he's smart and perceptive.

I flash a wicked smile. "Can we go now?"

He brushes a kiss across my lips. "Anytime, *printsessa*."

I relax and wrap my arms around him, pressing my face against his chest. He can't be bad.

He can't be.

I know my mom is wrong about him.

~

SASHA

MAXIM BUYS me a convertible Lamborghini Huracan in electric blue, which he says goes with my eyes. After we finish the paperwork and get the keys, he hands me into the driver's seat, his eyes ablaze with lust.

"Do I look hot?" I ask, remembering his words.

"Like a movie star." He walks around to the passenger side. I know it must kill him to ride shotgun. He's all alpha male. The guy who likes to drive, but he takes the seat with his casual grace.

I start the car, and we pull out of the lot, showing the paperwork at the gate. Rather than drive back to the apartment building, I just take off without any destination in mind. Maxim was right—I wanted the freedom.

Driving feels amazing.

Maxim doesn't comment or direct, another surprise. I push away my mother's voice in my head, reminding me he's just trying to keep me happy until he has my money.

"Did you want to be a movie star, Sasha?" Maxim asks.

"What?" I glance over and find he's examining me closely.

"You told Kayla you were jealous about her agent. How did that work out, anyway? Did you hear?"

Seriously? This guy is actually following up on my friend-gossip?

"She got the agent." Kayla texted me last night with the news.

"Good for her. So what about you, Sasha?"

I scoff. "Well, obviously, it's impossible."

"Because of me?"

"What?" I look over, surprised. "No. What chance do I have getting into even the smallest acting gig? I have a Russian accent. I need to lose thirty pounds. And yes, I don't live in L.A."

"What about acting here? Stage acting? Or even commercials."

I'm getting queasy. Maxim's words incite a riot of emotion in me. All the pent-up, stuffed-down hopes and dreams I've been harboring since I was a little girl. My dreams to act in a soap opera. A television show. Or yes, the stage. None of those have ever been a possibility. While I was at USC, I could pretend, I could dip my toes into the water and wish my future would be different, that I was someone else, but I knew it would come to an end.

"It's harder than you think," I snap, even though it's not his fault I'm getting flustered and upset. "And the accent's still a problem here."

"So we'll get you a speech coach. Lots of actors from other countries perfect an American accent. Look at Alicia Vikander, that Swedish chick from the last Bourne movie."

I blink, my nose getting hot. He's pushing at my resistance. The resistance I put up to protect myself from wanting this thing I can't have.

"I don't know how to even break into Chicago's theatre," I admit.

"Let's sign you up for acting classes. That will get you

into the scene. You'll meet people, find out about auditions. We can go check out all the local shows to get a sense of what's good and what's not."

One minute I'm driving down the road, the next minute, I'm sobbing.

"Sasha!" Maxim's alarmed voice cuts through the din in my ears. "Pull over, *lyubimaya.* Pull over here." Maxim indicates a turn and then another into a parking lot.

I stop the car and drop my forehead onto the steering wheel to bawl like a baby.

"Fuck. What did I say? Sasha? Look at me, sugar."

I try to look at him, but I'm totally falling apart. The definition of a hot mess. I don't even know why I'm crying. I'm not sad. I'm just totally overcome. "Nobody's ever supported my dreams," I choke, trying to see him through my tears. *"Nobody."*

I realize it's true. My mom wasn't a bad mom, but she was realistic. She taught me that arranging my life around a man was the only option. And her emotional energy was always taken up with my father. Of course, my dad forbade me to act in Russia and made it clear that I'd be coming home after college, and that would be the end of it.

My friends in college—well, they would never tear me down, but there was an element of competition. We all wanted the same thing, only they had a much better chance at it. *I* played the support role because I knew that path could never be for me.

"Do you… " It's hard to speak through my hiccups and sobs. "Do you really think I could act? I mean, you've never seen me."

"I *know* you can, sugar." He cups my face in his hands and thumbs away my tears. "There's nothing you can't do. You have crazy talent. You're smart. You're beautiful. And now you have a shit-ton of money at your disposal to create a support team. Nothing's going to stop you, *lyubimaya.*"

"I'm sorry," I croak. "I don't know why I'm crying. This is ridiculous."

"I'm sorry you weren't supported. But I've got your back now. We'll make it happen. Okay?"

I can hardly believe what he's telling me. Part of me still thinks he doesn't know what he's talking about. I mean, the theatre business is cut-throat. I can't just show up and say "I'm here" and get an acting job. But even the glimmer of hope—the idea I might even get to dabble. To play a tiny role in a tiny community theater—sounds better than nothing. Even at the very worst, I could use my money to become a patron of the theatre and be in the world as a benefactor.

I blink my tear-dotted lashes, peering at his handsome face. "Why would you want this for me? Doesn't it make me harder to protect?"

He shakes his head with total confidence. "No one will touch you. You're safe with me. I'll make sure of it. Living in Chicago isn't perfect for your career, but you can afford to fly out to L.A. if it gets to that. For now, getting started here might be exactly what you need. Who knows, right?"

"Wow." The sobs finally subside, and my breath calms. "I can't believe it."

"I'm sorry I didn't bring it up sooner."

I stare into his dark eyes, drawing strength from him. My whole world just changed. My reality flipped ass over teakettle a second time, only this time I couldn't be more overjoyed. It's like he just handed me a new shiny life on a platter.

"*Spasibo*," I whisper. *Thank you.*

He strokes his knuckles down my cheek lightly. "I told you there was nothing I wouldn't do for you."

I let out a watery laugh. "You told me that as an incentive to give you blowjobs."

He grins back and gestures to the car. "Look what it got you."

I shake my head, still not believing it. "Why are you being so nice to me?"

Maxim goes still. When he speaks, I'm certain the answer will be the truth. "Because you're mine," he says simply.

I blink rapidly. "Even though you didn't want me?"

He stares. There's no hint of a smile on his face. None of the casual, flippant charm. "I may not have wanted you when we married. But I want you now," he says with total seriousness.

I believe him.

"I may want you, too," I whisper, fresh tears glimmering in my eyes.

He lifts his chin toward the ignition. "Drive your new car. I like to see you happy."

I smile and start the car back up. "You're getting the best blowjob of your life tonight."

"Mmm." Maxim adjusts his cock in his pants, a smug look on his face. "I *do* like you on your knees."

CHAPTER 16

 asha

I'M LOUNGING on the couch watching *Game of Thrones* with Dima, Nikolai and Pavel. Maxim, Ravel and Oleg are off somewhere on business.

I haven't had much of a chance to talk to Lucy—she's always either at work or locked in the bedroom with Ravil, so when I see her walking to the door in a bathrobe and carrying a towel, I ask where she's going.

"To the rooftop pool." She rubs her belly. "It's my saving grace these days."

I shoot an accusing look at Nikolai and Pavel. "No one told me there's a pool on the roof."

"There's a pool on the roof," Pavel offers.

I smack him with the back of my hand and jump up. "May I join you?"

"Of course."

"Give me one minute," I say, shooting off for the bedroom to change into a bikini.

Pavel whistles when I come out with a towel wrapped around my waist, then winces. "I'm sorry. Please don't tell Maxim I did that. I don't want my dick cut off."

"Oh good. Something to hold over your head next time I want something from the kitchen." I smirk and head to Lucy.

She's blonde, probably ten years older than I am, and very serious. Not unkind but not the overly smiley type.

As we walk out, I mutter, "I can't believe no one told me about the pool. I know I'm under lockdown, but wouldn't that be safe enough?"

Lucy shoots me a sidelong glance. "How are you doing with the lockdown?"

"I'm sick of it." I shrug. "But honestly, I'm used to some degree of restriction. My father always had people following and watching me."

She leads me up a short flight of stairs and onto a beautiful rooftop with a hot tub and pool. Shade umbrellas and potted flowers and trees surround the pool, and there's a patch of fake grass. "And being married to Maxim? I heard that wasn't exactly your choice."

Or his. She leaves that part off.

At the side of the pool, she opens a box and pulls out a kick board, which she offers me.

I take it, and she pulls out a second one for herself.

"No, it wasn't. What did you hear?"

She hesitates. I gather she's the type who is too polite to speak about private matters. But I want to know what Maxim told the guys. What they think of me.

"I know you're the daughter of the boss in Moscow. And he arranged your marriage to Maxim."

"Yes." I follow her as she wades down the steps into the

pool. The water is nice—just cool enough to be refreshing, but not to shock my body or give me a chill. She tucks the kickboard under her chest and frog-kicks through the water. I do the same.

"It sounded like Maxim and your father were once very tight." She glances at me to verify. "And I understand they had a falling out, but Maxim was still loyal."

I nod. "I caused the falling out. Did you hear that part?"

"No. Ravil didn't mention the details, if he knows them."

Some of the pressure on my chest leaves. I should confess, but I'm too ashamed.

"I heard you didn't come here willingly, either."

"No," Lucy says. At the other end of the pool, she reverses her direction, this time using a flutter kick. "But Ravil grew on me. Maybe Maxim will grow on you, too."

"He's overbearing and dominant but actually way more of a gentleman than I expected." The memory of Maxim showing up in L.A. with a ring and letting me stay and party makes my heart squeeze almost painfully. He's better than I deserve. "I really thought he would string me up and eat my liver for breakfast."

"Things were that bad between you two?"

"Yes."

"Ladies." I look up to find Ravil standing at the edge of the pool, gazing at his girlfriend with adoration. He takes a seat in one of the chaise lounges to watch us as if we needed a lifeguard.

Lucy swims to the edge of the pool near him and deposits the kickboard. I join her.

"Have you heard from your mother, Sasha?" Ravil asks.

Warning bells go off in my head, and the hairs at the back of my neck stand up. "No," I lie. I still haven't been able to buy a burner phone because Ravil doesn't let me out of the house alone, but my mom has called and texted me from different phone numbers, always warning me to be careful of Ravil and Maxim.

I haven't spoken much with Ravil. If I'm honest, I'd have to admit he scares me. He's *pakhan*, like my father was. Even though he was technically under my father, I believe him to be just as powerful. That means men live and die by his orders.

He could have ordered Maxim to accept me as his bride because he wants control of Russian oil. He could have plans to kill me that Maxim doesn't know about. Or he and his Fixer could have worked out a plan together.

I don't want to think that way, but his question about my mother seems pointed.

He studies me in that way my father used to. Like he sees right through me.

I dip my head under the water to hide the fact that his stare unnerves me. When I come up, he's still watching.

"You don't know where she is?"

"Nope." I try to sound casual.

"It seems nobody knows where Galina went to," he tells me. "She disappeared at the same time Vladimir died."

My mouth goes dry. My heart pounds. I keep my lips pressed together to keep from filling the silence between us with information I shouldn't spill.

"Some people think she had something to do with his death."

"What?" This takes me by surprise. "That's ridiculous. Why—because she's gone? Of course, she's gone—it wasn't safe for her anymore without Vladimir's protection."

"His murder was strange. None of his enemies or potential successors claimed credit for it. And he was killed with poison—not really bratva style. Our form of murder is usually more… overt."

Lucy makes a sound of disapproval and swims away. I want to do the same, but I feel caught in Ravil's ice blue gaze.

"My mother didn't kill Vladimir," I say.

"You heard from her once, though, didn't you?" Ravil presses.

So Maxim *has* shared with him. Goosebumps prickle my skin, and I get queasy. I climb out of the pool. "I'm getting chilly," I say, not answering his question.

I grab my towel and wrap it around my shoulders. "Is Maxim downstairs?"

Ravil shakes his head. "No. But he'll be back soon."

More warning bells go off. I have to bite down to keep my teeth from chattering. I stuff my feet into my flip flops and manage to wave to Lucy before I make my escape.

I stumble down the stairs and into the hallway, stopping to lean against the wall outside the penthouse door. I wait for my heart rate to slow, but even when it does, even after I knock on the door to be let back in the suite, I can't shake the cold that's seeped into my veins.

SASHA

IT TAKES me four days before I can get a moment unsupervised. Maxim, Ravil and Nikolai went to some kind of meeting. I waited twenty minutes, then picked up my purse and headed for the door.

"Whoa, whoa, whoa," Dima says, catching Oleg's eye.

Oleg lumbers to his feet.

I hate the resentment that pops up toward them at keeping me prisoner. I like these guys. I felt like their equal. But now I have to ask permission to leave. Stuffing down my temper, I use my acting chops and hold up my hand like it's no big deal. "Just running to the drugstore on the corner. For girl stuff."

I don't know why talking about periods always makes men uncomfortable, but Dima and Pavel both look away. Oleg stands five feet away from me, clearly still ready to follow.

"Oleg should go with you," Dima says. He shrugs. "Maxim would kill us if we let you go out unprotected."

Again, I hide my irritation and shrug. "Suit yourself," I say to Oleg, holding the door open for him. We're silent in the elevator.

Well, duh. I'm silent. I do have the urge to make chit chat to fill the void, but I resist. I didn't ask for him to come along. I don't have to entertain. I walk to the corner drugstore. I turn and put a hand on Oleg's chest when he tries to follow me. "A little privacy?" I use my bitchiest bratva princess voice, but I'm instantly sorry, remembering what Ravil had told me. These guys don't work for me—they're his brothers. "I'm sorry, it's just… girl stuff." I wrinkle my nose. "Kind of embarrassing."

Oleg steps back and angles his back to the store, like he's going to guard the whole place while I'm in there.

"Thanks. I'll be out in a second."

He doesn't nod or acknowledge that I spoke at all.

I go in, quickly grabbing a pack of tampons and a few random cosmetics to fill a bag, and then I head to the electronics wall for a burner phone. It requires me getting help from an employee, which makes me nervous as hell because it takes me a minute to flag one down, and the wall is visible from the door. If Oleg looked in, he'd see us.

I keep my eye on his back, but he never turns.

Heart pitter-pattering, I make it through check out, the phone buried in the bag under my girly stuff.

I step outside, almost lightheaded with my success.

Mission accomplished.

"All set. Thanks for coming with me," I say, suddenly feeling quite chatty. "I'm sorry, I didn't mean to be rude. It just wears on me feeling like I never get space. But I know you guys are just trying to keep me safe, and I appreciate that."

Oleg slides his gaze over my way, but that's his only acknowledgement of my words.

"Do you need anything?" I ask, suddenly realizing how hard it must be for Oleg to function in this world. "Can I buy you a coffee or tea or anything?"

Oleg's brows come down and he shakes his head.

"Okay. How do you communicate when you want something, Oleg?" I come right out and ask him. He pulls his phone out of his pocket and holds it up. I blink, unclear what he's telling me. He obviously can't talk on the phone. Does he have some kind of app? "You text it?"

He tucks the phone away.

"Is that a yes? You can nod, you know."

His brows get lower.

"Sorry," I apologize. I know he won't hurt me, but he is pretty terrifying, just in sheer size and intimidation factor. The silent thing makes it even worse. I'm sure Ravil and his cell merely have to trot Oleg out with them and people piss their pants. "Was it a yes?"

He actually nods this time.

"Do you have my number?"

He frowns some more.

"So you can text me if you need something."

He shakes his head, but it's dismissive, like he's saying *no fucking way he'd text me for anything.*

I want to remind him that I'm the one who introduced him to his fantasy-girl, but that would be pushing it way too far. Befriending Oleg will probably be a long term project.

Back at the apartment, I go into the bedroom and then the bathroom, closing the door and running the bathtub for background noise. Then I call the last number my mom called from on the burner phone.

She doesn't answer at first, so I text that it's me and try again, and she picks up. "Sasha! How are you, darling?" she asks in Russian.

"I'm okay. Where are you?" I don't know why I fired that question off first. I guess it's because Ravil asked. Everyone seems to want to know her location.

"I'm somewhere safe."

"Why is she asking?" a gruff male voice rumbles in the background. The hairs on my arms stand up.

"Is that Viktor?"

"Yes. Where are you, Sasha? At Ravil's penthouse?" Later I would wonder how she knew about Ravil's penthouse, but my mind is already trotting forward to my most burning question.

"Yes. I'm in the bathroom with the tub running. That's the noise you hear."

"Where is Maxim?"

"I don't know—out on business. But he has roommates. They all live together on the top floor of a building. Mama…
"

"What is it, Sasha?"

164

"Um... " Asking your mother if she killed a man is harder than you'd think. "Who poisoned Vladimir?"

"Oh, probably Leonid," she says dismissively.

"But he hasn't claimed responsibility for the death. Ravil thinks that's strange. He made it sound like people think you did it," I blurt.

"Th-that's because he probably gave the order," my mother says, sounding flustered. I know her well enough to hear the thread of tension in her voice.

Warning bells go off, but I ignore them.

I don't want to believe my mom would do such a thing.

"Ravil has backed Kuznetsk. He's responsible for him taking the helm in Vladimir's absence."

That chill that I felt in the pool returns.

"Don't you see why, Sasha? If Vladimir's dead, he's one step closer to taking control of the oil wells. That's why I'm in hiding. As long as they can't find me, you're safe. You see? Because if you die, your money passes to me. But if we're both dead, Maxim and Ravil have it all. They take control of the money and the bratva. It's exactly what your father feared would happen to us."

I shake my head. "I-I think you're being paranoid, Mama," I tell her, but I can't stop the trembling in my hands.

"Have they asked about me? Did they ask you to find out where I am?"

I suck in a ragged breath. "They asked, but I said I didn't know. Which is true. So...I guess don't tell me. So I don't have anything to hide."

"I won't tell you. But how are you doing, darling? Are you a prisoner there?"

I think of what I just had to go through to buy the phone to call her. I expel a measured exhale. "It's a gilded cage, but yes. I'm a prisoner."

RENEE ROSE

"Has he hurt you?"

"Maxim?" Guilt seeps in through the cold. Am I wrong to listen to my mother? Maxim takes very good care of me—sexually and otherwise. How could I even think he planned to murder me? Besides, why would they need to murder me when they already control my money? I'm the one who should do the murdering around here. My father treated me like the spoiled princess he created, not trusting me to manage my own funds. Giving them to Maxim to divvy out to me as he sees fit.

It's ridiculous, really.

"No," I tell my mother. "He's good to me. I think you're wrong about them."

I hear Viktor say something in the background, but I can't make it out. "I have to go now," my mother says. "Call me again next week. I'm working on a plan to see you."

"You are?" I can't decide if that makes me happy or not. "Maxim said you could come here, and he'd protect you."

"I'd be crazy to trust him," my mother answers. "No, don't tell him you spoke with me."

"Okay, I won't."

"Promise me. It could mean my life."

Another wash of fear runs down the front of me. "I promise."

"I love you, daughter mine."

"I love you, too, Mama." I hang up, fighting the urge to burst into tears.

My mother is wrong.

She's wrong about all of it.

She has to be.

CHAPTER 17

Maxim

THERE ARE three things I adore about my new wife.

I love the sex. *Da*, that had to be first because nothing moves me like watching her surrender. Watching the walls and barriers between us crash down in a torrent of hot, brutal passion.

I also love the show. I love when she gets dolled up and turns her natural female magnetism way up. She's not afraid to talk to anyone. She loves to be the life of the party. She's the type people might call "too much," but I love every bit of it. In the week she's been here, she's already won over my roommates—even Lucy, and the two of them have very little in common, other than being female. She's won over the soldiers in the building—the doormen and guards. She's made friends with the baristas at the coffee shop on the corner. She knows how to work a room.

Most of all, though, I love when she shows me what's

167

really beneath it all. When she fell apart over acting. When we get real about her father. She's proud as hell, so I figure if she's showing me her weaknesses, it means something.

That she's mine in more than body and last name.

It still isn't all the time. She's mercurial. At times, I find her reserved and cagey—especially after I leave her alone for too long, but hopefully with time, she'll learn to trust that my attention won't be withdrawn the way her father's was.

Tonight she's all about the show. After our talk last week about theatre, she found a play to attend tonight. She's dolled up in a gorgeous open-backed blue designer dress, looking far more Hollywood star than her usual nightclub diva look. All the guys whistle when we emerge from the bedroom suite, and she tosses her red hair like a model on a runway.

"Where are you two headed?" Lucy asks from her stool at the breakfast counter. She's eating beef and potato perogies—her constant pregnancy craving.

"The Chicago Temple of Music and Art," Sasha answers. "Chicago Stage is doing *Cabaret*."

"Ooh, that will be good," Lucy says.

"That's a strip club, right?" Nikolai asks with mock innocence.

Sasha flips him the bird, and Dima chuckles.

"Are you taking the Lambo?" Pavel asks. "Or does Money Bags not let you drive?"

"The car was my gift to her, and it's my pleasure to let her drive," I answer smoothly.

Sasha beams. "You spoil me."

She drives to the theatre, and I direct her to the valet. When we get out, I slip a fifty in the guy's hand and tell him to take good care of it. He stumbles over himself thanking us and making promises.

Sasha rolls her eyes. "Man club."

"No. It's not because I'm a man." I show her the wad of fifties in my pocket. "It's a trick Ravil taught me—he read it in an old article in *Esquire Magazine*. It's called Twenty Dollar Millionaire. The theory was that you don't have to be rich to get respect or treated like a millionaire, you just need to grease palms. Flashing a twenty dollar bill will get you most anything. But with inflation, I figure it's fifties or hundreds now."

"I don't think that would work the same for a woman."

"Money gets you everything, *caxapok,* especially with the right attitude. And you have plenty of both. Don't play small when you could be so very big." I pull out a blank check I brought along and show her.

"What's that?"

"It's for the theatre company—if you wanted to get some attention with a donation. Make them remember your name."

I hand it to her, and she tucks it in her purse. I wouldn't say I'm a theatre guy. Yeah, okay, this is probably my first time—ever—seeing a live performance, but I enjoy it. I enjoy even more having Sasha on my arm turning heads. I enjoy her total absorption in the performance—the gasps and exclamations. Her standing ovation when it's over.

"That ending," she exclaims. "So powerful."

We hang back in the lobby. I know what I would do to make things happen for Sasha, but it's up to her.

"I'm going to find the director," she says.

I smile. "That's my girl. I'll be by the doors."

She finds me twenty minutes later, her eyes ablaze with glory. "I did it." She beams. "I used the donation check to get his attention, and then I told him I'm an actor who just moved here from Moscow. He invited me to his partner's acting class. It's on Tuesdays. And guess what?"

"What?"

"You're never going to believe this." She grabs my wrist and squeezes it, bouncing a little in her heels. "They're doing *Anna Karenina* next year, and he said he would love to have me audition for a part!"

I grin, trying to catch up. "They want a Russian in the part."

"Well, I don't know," she says quickly. "But at least my accent won't hurt me." She waves a business card in my face. "And I have a connection now."

I wrap my arm around her waist and pull her against my body. "You did it. See? There's nothing you can't do."

She kisses me in a flurry of happy pecks. "*Gospodi*, I love you!"

I swallow when the full brunt of those words hits me square in the chest.

She jerks back with a startled expression like she just did something wrong.

"I'm pretty nuts about you, too," I tell her before she can take it back.

Vulnerability bleeds into her expression, but she hides it. "Yeah?" She slides her hands up and down my chest. "I thought you married me for the money."

I go still. Is that what she thinks? "No. Your inheritance is a pain in my ass. The perk of this marriage isn't the money, sugar. It's you."

She steps in closer, tugging on my tie, insinuating her curves against my body. "You mean the sex."

I narrow my eyes, suddenly wary. I feel like Sasha's playing some role right now. The one her mother taught her about how to keep a powerful man. She's not being real with me. And feeling like I'm being played is a goddamn trigger for me, especially with her.

"I said *you*," I insist.

She catches the offense in my tone and pulls back slightly.

No, I misread her. I'm being a dick. She's fishing for confirmation that I feel the same. I capture her nape and tug her lips up to mine.

"Even the crazy parts. I love you, too, Sasha." It's awkward to say, but once the words come out, I'm not sorry. I'm as vulnerable as my bride. And that's what love is. Revealing your weakness. Trusting the other person with it.

She's given me that.

It's time for me to do the same.

"I love you," I repeat the words, staring straight into her blue eyes.

A shiver runs through her. "I used to fantasize about this moment," she whispers.

My lips kick up into a grin. "I annexed you out of all fantasies for fear of my life. But let me tell you, sugar—I'm making up for it now. I have about a hundred that involve you bent over that new car of yours."

"Oh yeah?"

I reach in my pocket for the valet ticket. "Want to go for a drive?"

Her smile is as wicked as my heart. She snatches the valet ticket from my fingers. "Always, big man."

SASHA

MAXIM DIRECTS me to one of those high rise parking garages that goes up and up and up. We take it all the way to the rooftop and park. There aren't any other cars up here. We get

171

out, and I walk to the wall to look over the edge at the city. "I love this," I exclaim.

It feels like the night belongs to us. It's all ours.

Maxim loves me. I can't—won't—stop that thought from swishing around me like a warm, bubblegum pink dream.

It feels too good to be true.

Like any minute, the relationship police are going to show up and arrest me for impersonating a real wife.

I mean, he had to marry me. He didn't even want me. How did I trick him into love?

How did he trick me?

Who is tricking whom?

Or is this actually real? It feels real, but I'm so afraid to trust in it. Everything seems too easy. Too perfect. Things looking up for my acting career. Living in the U.S. again, a short flight away from my friends. Making new friends in Maxim's roommates.

Feeling wild and celebratory and maybe with my exhibitionism coming out to play, I open the zipper on my dress and pull it over my head.

Rather than reaching for me, Maxim steps back and shoves his hands in his pockets, his gaze sweeping up and down.

"How was it you liked to punish me?" I purr, unfastening my bra. "Just in my heels?"

He pretends to be casual, but I see his erection tenting his pants. "Aw, fuck, sugar." He walks slowly toward me. "That teasing's going to get you spanked."

"Mm. I'm counting on it." I back up toward the Lambo, cracking the door to toss my dress and bra inside. He follows, keeping his distance and his relaxed posture.

I square off to him, holding his gaze as I slowly slide my g-string down my thighs and step out of it.

Maxim makes a beckoning motion, stepping closer. "I'll take those." I hand them to him, and he tucks them in his pocket.

"Hands on the hood. Spread your legs."

Thrills of excitement zing through me as I take the position, pressing both palms to the cool metal and affecting a wide stance in my high heels. It's a warm night, so I'm not chilled by my nudity out here. Or perhaps it's the heat pooling between my legs. The risk of being caught up here by someone, completely naked, makes this a hundred times more exciting than if we were somewhere private.

Maxim palms my breasts from behind, squeezing both nipples. "My wild bride." I toss my hair when I look over my shoulder at him. His hand claps down on my ass, hard. I shriek and then laugh. Tremors run down my legs.

"Ouch?" I murmur.

He slaps me on the other cheek, just as hard. "I know, *caxapok*. But you look so pretty with my hand prints on your ass."

More shivers shoot down my inner thighs, lifting my arches and curling my toes.

"Be a good girl and hold still for it." I do because I freaking love it. He spanks me in a flurry of short, quick slaps warming my ass with his palm until I'm shifting on my feet. "That's right." He rubs the sting away.

"What's it for?" I ask. I don't know why. I think part of me still wants to know if he's forgiven me for the past.

"For making me fall in love, *lyubimaya*."

I whimper because it tears me wider open every time he says it. Smashes my defenses. Leaves me more and more vulnerable to this man.

Did my father know I would feel this? That we could be happy together? In love?

Even the tiniest sliver of belief that he did feels like redemption. I didn't know I wanted to be redeemed. Certainly not by him. But the feeling is wonderful. He didn't despise me. What if he did want what was best for me?

"Please," I beg.

Maxim's fingers slide between my legs, and I almost come just from that touch. "Begging already, sweetness? You need my cock?"

"Yes."

"You want to be fucked over your brand new car? Need me to show you who's really driving around here?"

I laugh because I knew it must bother the extreme alpha male in him to let me drive, and yet he did it anyway. "Yes. Show me."

"I'll show you." I hear the rip of a condom foil, and then the head of his cock rubs over my wet folds.

I push back, eager to take him. After a week of non-stop sex, I'm addicted to the feel of him inside me. To coming when I'm stretched wide and sore from his pounding. Surrendered to his control.

He's a bossy lover. He talks dirty and puts me in degrading positions, but he always makes sure I come at least twice as many times as he does. He takes care of me.

He slaps my ass again lightly as he pushes in. "Damn," he groans. "You look like a *Penthouse* pinup right now, baby. You're like every man's dream. A hot car and an even hotter woman.

He reaches around to stroke my clit, easing in and out of me slowly. "What part do you like best, sugar? Your spanking or knowing we might be caught?"

"Getting caught," I gasp, my inner muscles squeezing his cock. Although I love the spanking, too. "You?"

"Me?" He catches hold of my hair and tugs my head back. "I just like being in charge."

I squeeze around him again.

"I like it when you offer yourself up to me like a gorgeous little fuck-doll." He pinches one of my nipples, then pushes my torso down. "Tits on the hood, beautiful."

The car is shiny clean, but even if it wasn't I would do what he told me. Maxim makes pleasing him a game I like to play.

He holds me down with his hand in the middle of my back and starts slamming in harder. When he pushes too hard and my pelvis slams against the car, I yelp and he instantly adjusts, wrapping his forearm in front of my pelvis to cushion the contact.

And then it's on.

He slams in harder and harder, making me lose my breath, lose my mind.

The pressure of wanting to finish before we're caught ratchets up my need, and yet it feels so good, I don't want it to be over, either.

"I'm going to fuck you up against the window at home. Out on the rooftop. I'm going to finger you in that theater the next time we go there."

"*Gospodi,*" I whimper. "I'm going to come."

"Not until I say." There's a sharp warning in his voice.

He hasn't played this game with me before, and I go cross-eyed, trying to hold back the tidal wave about to descend.

"You be a good girl and wait for permission."

"You're… crazy," I pant.

He grips my hair, pulling my head back at the same time he pushes my torso down, making me arch for him. Hurting

175

me lightly in that wonderful, dominant way of his. "Crazy for *you*."

He comes, and I screech, already coming, too, unable to hold off any longer. Maxim chuckles darkly, dropping his torso down over mine, his cock still inside me, his body molded to mine from the back. "You'll be punished for that, *lyubimaya.*"

I close my eyes, my internal muscles pulsing again around his cock in an aftershock. "I couldn't help it."

He kisses my neck. "Me either."

CHAPTER 18

 asha

I WALK out of my acting class with a group of actors, still talking about the Stanislavaski exercise we did. It's the third week I've been going, and I already feel like I belong. I have friends. I love the exercises. I'm getting the inside scoop on the Chicago scene.

Maxim found a Hollywood speech coach to help me with my accent in virtual sessions, and if I concentrate, you can barely tell I'm not American. At least, that's what my new friends say.

"Hey Sasha, you want to join us for coffee?" one of the older women asks.

I hesitate.

At first, Maxim didn't want to let me come to this class alone, but I threw a fit. Having a possessive and protective husband sitting in on class would make everyone think I was a freak. After a throw-down, he ended up dropping me off and picking me up for the first class, but last week, he decided I could start leaving the Kremlin on my own because Dima's new data mining program is in place, and things are settling down in Moscow.

It finally gave me the chance to pick up a burner phone and call my mom, who still wouldn't tell me where she is. I felt a little guilty breaking my promise to only go straight to class and home and hiding the phone and the conversation from him, but my mom was still full of suspicions about Maxim's intentions, which made me wary.

Am I still in danger? Or is the only real danger from him? I don't really believe it, but I don't want to be foolish, either. I read every Agatha Christie book as a child. I know large sums of money make people untrustworthy.

"Not this time," I say. It's not just my promise to Maxim. It's that the chef was going to cook a nice meal, and we were all going to eat together tonight. And as much as I want to make new friends, especially actors, I'd rather get to know and hang out with my new family.

I walk to the parking lot next to where my class is held. No valet nearby, unfortunately. Parking the Lamborghini in an unattended lot made me nervous, and I'm so relieved to see it's still there.

I open the door and slide in, tossing my purse on the seat beside me. When the door opens back up, I shriek in surprise.

"Get out, the car is going to blow," she says in clipped Russian.

"Mama?"

"Get out, now." My mother drags me out of the car and pulls me, ducking low, at a run through the rows of parked cars.

An explosion knocks me forward. I think I scream.

Even though she told me it was going to blow, I'm in disbelief. I turn to stare at the smoke and flames.

My mother yanks me forward until we reach an alleyway, and then she pulls me into it.

"Mama! What's happening"

She doesn't answer, just keeps yanking me along, down the alley, up a side street, back around until we're on the other side of the street, the sirens of police and fire trucks shrieking as they race to the scene.

We go into the hotel across the street and straight for the elevators.

Tears drip down my face. "What's happening? Who did that?"

"It's all right, darling." My mother turns to face me in the elevator and takes both my hands. To my surprise, she looks happy. Giddy, almost. "We did that!"

"Wh-what?"

My mother nods, beaming. "Viktor set the bomb. You're free now!"

It must be the reverberation of the bomb because a ringing in my ears suddenly makes me deaf. In a bubble of confusion and shock, I don't hear the elevator ding or notice the doors open, but my mom tugs me out of it and into a hotel room. Alexei sits on one of the double beds watching television. Viktor stands at the curtain watching the mayhem below. He gives me a curt nod.

I run to the window to look down at my sweet car—my beautiful baby that Maxim bought me because I'd look hot in —but it's completely gone. Viktor grabs my upper arm and yanks me roughly back, jerking my shoulder and giving my neck whiplash.

"*Kakogo cherta*?" I snap in Russian. *What the hell?*

"Keep her away from the window," he orders my mother,

like I'm not even worth explaining things to. His words sound far away, filtered through the echoing in my ears.

I stare at his handprint on my arm in shock. "What did you do?" I ask my mother.

She cups my face. "I killed you. You're dead now. You're free of Maxim and Ravil and their plans for your money. Now it all goes to me—to us!"

"Us?" I ask.

My stomach drops out. My body turns ice cold. I think I always knew my mom had money issues. She loved money but was terrified of losing it. That's why she put up with my dad—to be kept in luxury. And then her worst fears manifested when he left Vladimir in control of her purse strings. I knew she had these fears, but now I suddenly see her through a new lens. Like when the wicked witch in a fairytale—the one who was beautiful and said all the right things—is suddenly unveiled as an ugly old hag.

"D-did you kill Vladimir?" I ask.

She turns away when she answers, "Don't be ridiculous," and I know at once it's a lie. She did it. Maybe not personally, but she was a part of it. My mother and these two men, Viktor and Alexei, were somehow responsible.

I want to cry, but no tears come out. I'm in too much shock.

"You didn't have to do this. Maxim would've taken care of you," I say weakly. I think it's true. She sowed all that doubt—she's the one who was conniving.

My mother whirls back, anger marring her pretty face. "Would he? I doubt that. This is a man who tried to rape you when you were seventeen."

I shake my head, nausea hitting my belly. I'm just as bad as my mom. Cut from the same cloth. Taking stupid, desperate measures to prove I'm not as powerless as I feel.

"He didn't. I lied about that. I offered myself, and he refused." It feels horrible to say it out loud.

I barely get the words out, but they turn all the heads in the room—Alexei lowering the volume on the television as he stares at me. "What a bitch," he mutters, shaking his head and looking away.

"I wondered why Igor married her to him," Viktor snorts. "He must've known."

"Well, Maxim won't get his consolation prize after all," Alexei says.

"Too bad for him." Viktor looks down at the scene below. "Here he is now."

I rush to the window. Viktor throws out an arm to stop me from getting too close, but I see the scene unfolding below.

Maxim's Conquest Knight is parked askew at the end of the police barricade. Ravil and Oleg are still climbing out, but Maxim is running down the sidewalk, a cop chasing him. When he gets to the scene and sees the wreckage—the residue of what used to be my car and the two cars parked near mine only partially extinguished by the firemen on the scene—he drops to his knees.

His fists punch the air, his head drops back. I see his mouth open in a howl of rage, and in that moment, I swear I feel his pain like my own.

Like I'd just lost my one true love.

Him.

I don't think—I just move. "I'm going down there."

Fuck this. Fuck my mom and her stupid plan to get me free of Maxim. I don't want to be free. I want him in charge of me and my life and my money. I want him looking out for me, protecting me. Insanely possessive of me.

He's my man. He's always been the one.

Viktor grabs me by the hair and yanks me back. I have to

frantically stutter step backward to keep from falling on my ass and losing a whole chunk of hair in the crash.

"You're dead now," he growls. "You have to stay dead. What do you think Ravil and his cell will do to your sweet mother if they find out what she planned?"

What *she* planned?

My heart thunders in my chest.

"Viktor!" my mother snaps.

I look at her in disbelief. *This* is what she brought on us? She thought I'd rather be owned by Viktor over Maxim?

She basically sold us both out to Igor's lowest two-bit thugs. How long does she think they'll let us live before they take all the money for themselves? Does she think she can keep Viktor entertained on her back with her legs spread forever?

I doubt she can.

I don't know if I'm satisfied or dismayed to see her flicker of fear at the way Viktor's roughing me up. The color drains from her face.

We are both so fucked.

But then she rallies. "Let her go! It's fine! I can handle her, you don't have to," she soothes him.

Viktor yanks my hair harder. *"You stay dead. Do you understand?"*

"Yes," I gasp. "I'll stay dead," I say.

He still doesn't let go of me.

My mother draws herself up. *"Viktor."*

"I'll stay dead!" I repeat.

He releases me and shoves me away from him. My mother catches me, and even though her face is a mask of soothing, I note the trembling in her hands.

Tears burn my eyes and throat. Unwilling to cower and hide, I turn back to the window, my gaze glued to Maxim.

Ravil and Oleg haul him to his feet and hold him up as a ring of police officers surround them.

Maxim. Gospodi, I'm dying for him. If I were in his shoes thinking he'd been blown up, my heart would be torn in pieces.

And in the darkness of all that, creeps a tiny sliver of light.

He *did* care.

My mother was wrong about him.

He was down there on his knees over losing me.

If I could somehow get out of here and get to him, I could end that pain.

But what if Viktor's right? What if Ravil retaliates against my mother for scheming to take the money away from them? But I could beg for her life. I could make them see. If I went back, they'd still have the money.

Except my stomach goes queasy at all the uncertainties there. Would I even be welcome back after my mother staged this coup and apparently the one in Moscow against Vladimir? Would they have to kill her now to settle scores on both continents?

My eyes burn, but I blink the tears back. I'm an actress, and it's never been more important that I hide my emotions.

My mother gathers herself and comes over to me, clasping my arms and smiling into my face like I didn't just get assaulted by her boyfriend. "This is the perfect arrangement, Sasha. You will see. As soon as I get control of the money, we can live the rest of our lives on a beach in the Canary Islands. All that money, ours."

Dream on, Mama. I fear she's just lying to herself now. She must realize how tenuous her hold on Viktor is. How dangerous he might turn out to be. How screwed we are. But she's set this plan in motion, and there's no going back on it.

For any of us.

"You won't ever have to answer to that man who hates you again," she promises.

That man who hates you.

Yes, I believed Maxim hated me. The day my father died I was sure of it. But not anymore. He'd dropped his grudge even before I gave my virginity to him. He'd let me play brat —flying to L.A. and making him chase me—and he hadn't even been angry. His punishment had been delicious. He'd brought me a wedding ring and played nice with my friends.

He bought me a car.

Helped me find my way in the theatre scene.

Took me out and shared his friends with me.

All I'd done was make his life difficult and let him fold me over the hood of my car for hot sex.

If I make it out of this alive, I'm going to be the most grateful wife a man could ever have.

But it's a big *if.*

And I'm not about to use the skills my mother modeled on another man. I owe Maxim that much. If I get myself out of this, it won't be using my femininity as a weapon.

It will have to be my brains.

Maxim

I CAN HARDLY SEE, hardly think with the pounding behind my eyes. It feels like the center of my head will split open.

My chest already has. I left my organs—my fucking heart —out on that sidewalk in front of the parking lot.

"Who killed her," I rage back at the penthouse.

Dima's working like a maniac, his head down, his fingers flying over keys. I'm about an inch from severing his head from his shoulders over this. His fucking program was supposed to keep her safe. Alert us to anyone coming into the country.

"I'm analyzing everyone who came in before the program was in place," Dima says quickly, shoulders hunched. Nikolai stands behind him looking at the screen as well. Possibly to protect his twin from me when I lose my shit.

"There." Nikolai points at the screen. "What about that one? One male entering San Francisco from Moscow two weeks ago."

Dima shrugs and taps away at the keyboard, fingers flying even faster.

"Can you get scans of passenger's passports?"

"I'd have to hack a database. That will take time."

"I want a name now!" I thunder.

Sasha will be avenged. Blood will be spilled. By tonight, if I have my way.

"Hack in on the Russian side," Nikolai advises in a low voice. "Haven't you been in there before?"

Dima bobs his head and taps away some more. Ten minutes later, Nikolai shouts, "There! I know him."

"Who is it?" I demand.

"Alexei Preobrazhensky," Dima reads. "Lived in Moscow. In the same building as Galina and Sasha. Must've been a guard?"

I stomp over to look at the photo. "Mother. Fucker. He's a dead man now."

"He's a nobody," Ravil says. "This is not his operation. Whoever has Galina must've sent him to do the dirty work."

I glare at Dima. *"Find him."*

Dima shoots a helpless and stressed look at Ravil, but

then returns his focus to his screen. "Checking domestic flights to Chicago under the false alias."

I pace the living room.

"Put that away in here," Ravil commands.

I hear his words but I'm not listening.

"Maxim."

I look over.

"I said put that away." He lifts his chin in the direction of my hand.

I look down to find I'm palming my gun. The safety is off.

Fuck. I put the safety back on and shove the piece in my waistband. "Give me something, Dima. If I don't put a bullet between this guys eyes tonight, I will fucking lose it."

Oleg stomps over to me. He stands at least a head above me, his shoulders half again as wide as mine.

"What?" I snap.

He drops a giant ham-hand on my shoulder and then lowers his head.

If it were anyone else, I'd probably punch him, but Oleg so rarely tries to communicate, I force myself to receive his condolences.

But it's a mistake. I suddenly can't breathe, grief tearing at my throat, making my eyes burn. I wheeze and drop my hands to my thighs, trying to draw a breath.

Fuck. Sasha's dead.

My beautiful, smart, funny, lively, incredible wife is dead.

She'll never brighten this room again with a smart remark. Never toss that red mane of hers. I'll never get to see her act.

I never saw her act!

I try and try, but I still can't breathe. My heart pounds, my throat's closed tight like a fist.

I want to die.

Yeah.

Living without her isn't worth it.

So I let myself choke out. I stop trying to breathe and stumble to one knee. My head hits the coffee table on the way down. The blackness that follows is relief.

CHAPTER 19

asha

"I'M HUNGRY. Are you guys hungry? Should we order up some room service?" I decide the best course of action is to playact with my mother that I'm on board and everything is perfect. Until I figure out what my options are and what I can do.

I still desperately want to get to Maxim, to ease his heartache. I want to believe that he'll take me back and somehow save my mother from her folly.

But I suspect even if Maxim took me back, my mother's life would be forfeit. And as much as I hate her for this terrible plan, it's not enough to want her dead.

Right now I'm the definition of stuck between a rock and a hard place.

"Alexei will get takeout," Viktor says. "Right, Alexei?"

"Great." Sending Alexei out sounds like a stupid idea to

me considering the cops are still out there, but I don't argue. I'm pretending to be agreeable. And I really am hungry.

"Mama do you have a nail file?" I try to sound casual. I don't have a phone, but maybe I could get a hold of my mom's. Just to let Maxim know I'm alive. That I love him. That this wasn't my plan.

Of course, I don't even know the man's number! It was programmed in my phone, which went up in flames in the car, along with the burner phone and everything else in my purse.

My mom produces her purse from one of the dresser drawers and hands me a nail file. I pretend to file my nails as I eyeball the contents of the purse. I don't see a phone but that doesn't mean it isn't in there.

"I don't have a toothbrush," I muse.

"We can buy all of those things," my mother says. "Alexei will get one when he's out. And tomorrow we'll leave for Russia."

Russia. That makes my stomach twist into an even tighter knot.

Farther away from Maxim. From my heart.

"Do you have a passport for me?"

"*Da.* We have everything," my mother says. "Once we are in Russia, I will hire an attorney to get our money. Then we'll be free forever, Sasha. You and me."

You, me and two guys I don't trust an inch not to off the both of us when we get the money.

Although Viktor does seem to care for my mother.

Alexei turns off the television and stands. "All right. I'll get the food." He walks out the door without asking what anyone wants.

Asshole.

Also—duh. Of course he's an asshole. An asshole who

190

probably wouldn't hesitate to put a hole in my head if I don't pretend I'm totally on board.

At first, I thought the worst. That I'd be lucky if I made it out of this hotel room. But the more I think through it, the more I realize that might not be true. I have to remember— they *didn't* kill me down there. And they could have. So my mother is running this show. She does have sway over Viktor and Alexei, or else, I'd already be dead.

I remember how Viktor looked at her in my apartment after my father died. He definitely had a thing for her. So while he may be willing to kill me, I don't think he actually plans to unless I press his hand.

Or at least not until he has my mother's money. This crazy plan doesn't work without her. Maybe he really is dreaming of living out the rest of his life on the Canary Islands with my mother at his side.

Alexei returns with styrofoam containers of Italian food— ravioli and linguini. I sit cross-legged on one of the beds and pick at my container of noodles. My mom comes and sits beside me, shoulder to shoulder, like we're on some kind of family vacation.

As if we ever stayed in a hotel this dumpy in the past.

"Mama," I murmur. "You should have told me your plan."

"It was safer this way, darling," she says.

Safer.

Gospodi. I don't want to be safe. I want to be with Maxim. And now she's ruined that.

Even though I'm starving, the food seems to sit like a rock in my belly. After a few bites I just stir the contents around.

I'm about to get up and throw the rest away when the door bursts open.

～

Maxim

"THEY'RE MINE," I snarl before Pavel slides the keycard we stole from housekeeping through the slot in the door.

I've never wanted to spill blood more. They took from me the only thing I've ever had worth keeping. The only thing precious to me.

I don't even know how to grieve her. I just want to obliterate everyone who had anything to do with her death from the planet.

I screwed a silencer on my gun. The moment I kick open the door I find a head to point it at and shoot. Alexie dead. Viktor dead.

"Hold." Ravil grabs my wrist and swings my arm toward the ceiling when I turn to aim and shoot the next asshole on my list. "Maxim."

My brain stutters in shock.

There, on the bed, sits my beautiful bride. Very much alive. Sitting beside her mother, eating pasta from a container like I didn't just have my fucking heart ripped out.

Fuck.

Me.

Fuck me, fuck me, fuck me, fuck me.

No.

This can't be.

I shake my head slowly from side to side in disbelief.

She...*played* me?

Again?

She fucking played me.

Lied and betrayed me again.

This—this burns even worse than her death.

So much worse. Because if she was dead, I would at least have had her memory to nurture. To hold and remember and treasure until the day I died.

But this?

This I definitely won't come back from. Not with any shred of humanity or trust left in me. I thought women were untrustworthy before, but I will never be able to touch a woman again without tasting the ash of betrayal in my mouth.

"Maxim," she croaks, slowly lowering the container of pasta.

"Don't speak to me," I order, and then I turn and walk out, leaving Ravil to do my job as a fixer and clean up the holy mess I left behind.

CHAPTER 20

SHOCK MADE me freeze when Maxim came in. Seeing him so deadly—gunning down Viktor and Alexei with military precision, a bullet right between their eyes—stunned me.

And it demolishes my heart because he's doing it for me —avenging my supposed death.

I want to run at him and throw myself in his arms... until Ravil stops him from pointing the gun at me, and I see the betrayal on his face. The color drains from it. His eyes go dead. He shakes his head, his gaze on me murderous.

That's when my heart stops beating altogether.

Not physically, but emotionally.

The man I love—the only man I've ever loved—the only man who's ever loved me now hates me.

He believes I duped him. The shreds of our existence flutter down around my ears, forming a terrible, horrible pattern.

His mother—lying to him about coming back.

Me—telling lies about him to get him banished.

And now this—what must seem like the biggest betrayal of all.

He must believe it was all fake. All a lie. That I played along until I had my chance to steal my fortune away from him. Leaving him heartbroken and alone.

And me sipping Mai Tais on a beach in Spain with my mother.

Neither my mother nor I made a peep during the shooting. No screams. No movement. It's like we're the prey animals whose only protection is going perfectly still.

"Maxim." I finally make my voice work, force my lips to move.

"Don't speak to me." He turns and leaves the hotel room, taking my life—my future—everything I ever wanted and more—with him.

Ravil, Pavel and two soldiers I don't know crowd in the room.

It takes me a few seconds to realize Ravil's gun is still out, and he's considering me and my mother. I remember my mom orchestrated Vladimir's death, and Ravil must know that.

"Ravil," I croak. "It was them." I point at the dead men on the floor. Men I can't find it in me to feel one ounce of sadness for. I don't believe my mother cares much, either. "My mother and I are the victims here." Now I've become the liar Maxim believes me to be.

"Hvatit vrat!" Ravil barks. *Enough with the lies.*

I drop the pretense and do the only thing I can think to do to save her life—I beg.

"Please don't kill her…us… *please.*"

Ravil seems to make up his mind. He tucks his gun in the waistband of his slacks. "It's for Maxim to decide."

The air leaves my lungs. Maxim will decide our fate. Whether we live or die. I honestly can't decide if that's a good or bad thing.

Does he hate me enough to condemn us to death?

Ravil gives orders to the soldiers with him, and they start to move around, staging the bodies. "You two—get your things." He beckons to us.

We scramble up off the bed. My mother grabs her purse and zips up a small suitcase.

To Pavel, the *pakhan* says, "Get them out of here and into a different hotel. Sit on them until I contact you."

Pavel nods wordlessly. He doesn't look at me when he walks past. "Let's go."

We leave the dingy hotel room, and Pavel leads us down the stairwell and out a back door to the alley behind the hotel.

"I didn't know, Pavel," I try to tell him as we follow his long strides. "This wasn't my plan."

"Save it." He affects a cold, bored tone.

My heart thuds painfully against my sternum. "I got in my, car and my mom pulled me out, and then it blew. That was the first I knew about this."

"I don't give a shit about your story, Sasha. Save your breath."

Hot tears burn the backs of my eyes. "I need to talk to Maxim."

That seems to get under his skin. He stops and whirls. "No, you don't," he snaps. "You don't ever need to talk to him again."

My tears start to fall in earnest.

"You don't fucking deserve the tears he shed over you."

My heart squeezes so tight it stops beating for a moment. Maxim cried over me?

Pavel throws open the door to a white Mercedes SUV, and my mom and I climb in the back.

"This wasn't my plan," I repeat brokenly as he starts the car.

"Shut your mouth, Sasha," Pavel says. "Or—" he breaks off and shakes his head.

He probably left the threat unspoken as a fear tactic, but the silliest part of me wants to believe it's because Maxim loves me. And Pavel can't threaten me in case we work things out.

I cling to that hope for the drive.

My mother says nothing. Her face is drawn up and pinched, and she squeezes my hand tightly, but doesn't say a word.

She probably knows how much danger our lives are in.

Pavel takes us to another seedy hotel, and we follow him in. After he books a room with two doubles, he lets us in it, and sits down in the chair.

When he takes out his gun and rests it on his knee I give up on conversation.

In fact, I give up on figuring any part of this out. I pull back the covers to one of the beds, crawl in and squeeze my eyes closed.

If only I could fall asleep and forget it all.

~

Maxim

. . .

I STUMBLE INTO THE PENTHOUSE, which appears to be spinning. I thought I waited long enough, drinking straight vodka at the bar on the corner, that everyone would be asleep, but no fucking luck.

It's like the assholes were waiting up for me.

And the sympathetic vibe makes me want to hurl.

"Fuck off, all of you." Not sure if I growled it in Russian or English. Maybe Chinese.

I stumble, and Nikolai gets up like he's going to help me, so I take a swing at him.

And miss.

And somehow end up on my face, my shoulder smacking the couch on my way down.

Oleg hauls me to my feet. At least I think it's Oleg. No one else could do it so easily.

I blink up at him. "Fuck off," I slur.

I'm not sure what happens after that. I think I black out.

When I become aware of my surroundings again, light's pouring through the windows straight into my skull. I try to move and roll off the couch onto the floor.

All the fucking assholes are still in the living room. Or maybe they left and came back, I can't be sure.

I climb up and sit on the couch. "What do you want?" I grumble at Dima, who gazes at me from his work station.

"I'm sorry about Sasha," he says.

I want to kill him for saying her name.

I hold up a finger. "Don't ever say that name to me again."

Ravil plops down next to me. "Just one more time."

My head seriously feels like it's been split in half with a hatchet.

"Pavel is sitting on Sasha and Galina. What do you want to do with them?"

My lip lifts in a snarl at hearing her name again. My stomach lurches. What do I want to do with her? My first thought is to put them both in a tower on a remote island where they can never trick another man.

It could be a luxurious tower. Somehow, despite my pain, I still want her to be comfortable.

And safe.

Because on a remote island, all the sharks who want that money wouldn't be able to find them.

But that isn't my problem now. I honored Igor with my promise, and now his daughter is dead.

By her own choice. My obligation to protect her is over.

Why, then, do I still feel the urge?

I scrub a hand over my face. The stubble on my jaw scratches my palm. "Let them go. Tell them to never show themselves again to any of us. The responsibility for their actions is theirs alone. I wash my hands of it." I meet Ravil's gaze for the first time. "You should, too."

He nods. "If that's what you want."

"It is."

"I'll call Pavel. What do you want me to tell Moscow?"

"Tell them... " I rub my forehead. "Tell them Sasha's dead." I shrug. I have to protect her that much. They will probably still hunt down Galina, but this way if Sasha separates from her mother, she might live. "Don't tell them we know any differently."

"All right." Ravil stands. "We cleaned the mess at the hotel."

I stand, feeling like I weigh a million pounds. "Thanks."

I stagger into my room. Being in the space I shared with Sasha hits me like a semi-truck. I want to throw everything she owned out the window. Instead, I grit my teeth and pack her shit up—as much as I can fit in the two suitcases she came here with, and then I toss them out of my room.

Nikolai, Dima and Oleg stare at me. "Will one of you bring those to her?" I mutter.

Nikolai's brows lift. He must still be feeling sorry for me because he stands right up. "Yeah. I'll bring them now. Clear this shit out of here."

"Thanks." I stomp back into my room and get in the shower.

That's the end of it.

I'm over her now.

I'm over all women.

I will never, ever trust a single word that comes out of a woman's mouth again.

CHAPTER 21

asha

WE'RE NOT at the type of hotel with food service, but Pavel orders delivery of donuts and coffee. I think they're mostly for himself, but he got a half dozen, and after eating, he tosses the bag onto the bed where my mother and I are still huddled.

He didn't sleep in the bed. I'm not sure he slept at all, but he doesn't look tired. He looks exactly the same. Indifferent. Casual. Lethal. So jaded for a man so young.

We spent the morning in silence. I'm too afraid to appeal to him again, like I'm afraid of using up my only chance to fix this.

Is it even fixable?

The dread in my gut tells me no, but I can't accept that.

Pavel's phone rings, and he answers it. "Yeah. Got it." He stands. "Nikolai is bringing your shit, and I'm leaving. You're on your own. Maxim says you can stay dead and keep your

203

fortune, as long as neither of you ever show your faces to anyone in this cell again. Got it?"

I stand up. "No."

He cocks his head, disbelief and scorn mingling on his expression. "No?"

Now that I know they don't intend to kill my mother, I can finally move. Can finally function and make a choice. "I need to see Maxim and explain things. I don't want to stay dead. I want to go back."

"Sasha!" my mother barks. "What are you doing?" She also climbs off the bed, walking around behind me.

For as long as I can remember, my mom has made me believe she's done everything for me. That she and I were on the same team, conspiring against the outside world. Against the men. Growing up, she made sure we were well taken care of, and she also made sure I knew it was through her efforts.

She showed me all her tricks. Explained why she needed me to be a good little girl and wait in my room while she seduced my father again and again, night after night. When I was older, why I should stop asking him to let me go to America for college. Why I needed to act more like her.

For whatever reason, I rebelled against my father, but I never rebelled against her. I guess she made it seem like she and I were in the same boat.

Now, for the first time in my life I take a stand against her. "It was *my* money, Mama." The words sound awful to my ears, and my mother recoils, but it's the truth. My father didn't trust me with my inheritance, so he gave it to Maxim. Now my mother's taken it from me.

And if I had to choose between being controlled by Maxim or my mom… I'd take Maxim any day.

"You told me Maxim and Ravil wanted to steal it, but you were the one who wanted to take it from me."

My mother slaps me across the face, hard.

My eyes smart, and Maxim's words come back to me, like a horrible taunt—a bitter reminder of what I've lost.

No one will ever slap your face again—this I promise you. Not if they want to live.

"I did this for you, you ungrateful brat!" My mother snarls. "We could have killed you for real in that car." She jabs a finger at me. "*That's* how I would take your money, if that had been my desire. It would've been far more simple. And Viktor would still be alive for me to enjoy it with!"

I stare at her, fighting back the weight of grief that washes over me. Not from this conversation, but from a lifetime of knowing subconsciously that my mother truly didn't love me, except as an extension of herself. That I was a pawn in her game against Igor for his money. Nothing more.

She spreads her arms wide. "I did this for *you*. To free you of that man."

"I didn't want to be freed of him!" I shout. I look desperately toward Pavel, who stands at the door looking like he wants to leave but is incapable of looking away from this trainwreck between my mother and I.

"Please, you have to tell him. It wasn't me. I didn't want this."

Pavel shakes his head in disgust. "I'm not telling him anything," he says and walks out the door.

My mother turns and grabs her suitcase. "Let's go. We have a flight to catch to Moscow."

I can't seem to move. I've never felt so lost or alone in my entire life. The desire to sink down into it—to gripe, complain, rebel—all the old stale tricks of my childhood surface, but I see how completely useless they are.

Maxim was right—power isn't something someone grants you. It's something you take for yourself.

"I'm not going."

My mother freezes and then slowly pivots. "What?"

"I'm not leaving my husband."

"Did you not hear? Your husband said if we ever show our faces again, they will strip us of the money." She gestures with both hands. "*We can't live without that money!*"

"Look at you," my mother scoffs. "You've never had a job in your life. What would you do? How would you live? And for what purpose? Maxim isn't going to take you back. I saw his face when he saw you were alive. You betrayed him once. You're lucky he didn't choke the life out of you right there for betraying him a second time."

I wave my fists in the air like a lunatic. "I did not betray him a second time! *You* did! And I will make him see that."

My mother's eyes go wide. "Are you insane? You would wish us both dead, then?" She takes a step back, pretending to be hurt.

I suddenly see where I got the acting gene.

"Or just me?"

"No, Mama. He's not going to kill you. He would've already done it. He spared you because he cares about me. That's the part you missed. Maxim and I were falling in love. He bought me that car!" I gesture to the street as if my car was still out there and not blown into a billion pieces. I use the car as an example because money is all that matters to my mother. Of course, to me, it wasn't the car. It was how he looked at me in the car. How he said it matched my eyes. How he wanted to fuck me over the top of it. How he liked to spoil and then disrespect me in equal measures.

"I saw his face," my mother says stubbornly. "He won't forgive you."

I straighten my spine. He forgave me once. I think he

could do it again. Hopefully it won't take eight years to heal this time.

"You go to Russia. I'm staying here."

My mother puts down the suitcase. "I'll wait. When he rejects you, we'll go together."

I don't pretend she wants to be here with me. She's staying because if I go back to Maxim, if I declare myself undead, the money is mine again.

Not hers.

When she was talking about being penniless, she was afraid for herself. With Vladimir alive, she would've been given a monthly allowance. Now that she killed him, she'll get nothing. In fact, she's probably not safe in Moscow at all. I don't know if Vladimir had many friends, but it seems like someone would want her blood for what she did.

A knock sounds on the door. I walk to open it, but my mother whisper-snaps, "Wait!"

"What?" I whisper-shout back.

"Just because he said we're free to go doesn't mean we really are."

I open the door a crack. It's Nikolai with my suitcases. As soon as he sees me, he turns and walks away.

"Wait!" I call. "Please. I need to talk to Maxim."

"That's not going to happen, *printsessa*," Nikolai says.

"He's my husband," I insist, as if that will mean something to Nikolai, who is already three-quarters of the way down the hall to the elevator.

"He's a widower." Nikolai doesn't even turn as he speaks the words. And then he steps into the elevator and is gone.

Dammit.

I've never hated myself so much in my life. I did everything wrong with Maxim. My stupid, cruel lie about him trying to force me into sex as a teenager. Acting like a spoiled brat when he brought me here.

And I don't know what I could've done differently with my mom, but I wish I'd done it. I shouldn't have bought the burner phone and told her about my acting class. I shouldn't have let her sow all that doubt about Maxim. I should have told her—convinced her—that I was happy with him. Then she wouldn't have made this desperate move.

The one that just ruined my life along with hers.

I choke back a sob as I wheel my suitcases into the hotel room. "I have to see him," I say.

My mother blocks my path. "We don't have any money, Sasha. No credit cards, no cash. Nothing."

"How did you get here?"

"Viktor," she whispers.

Right. Viktor. Who is dead. My credit card—courtesy of Maxim—was blown up with my purse.

I have no phone. I can't even take an Uber to the Kremlin.

"We need to use those plane tickets and get back to Moscow. Then we can get your money and a fresh start."

Here she goes again with her big plan.

"Mama, it takes months to transfer property after a death. Maxim didn't even have access to Igor's money yet."

Her face goes pale. "That's our only hope."

It's hers.

But not mine.

My hope is Maxim. My life is Maxim. I just have to get him to see me, so I can make him believe.

I open my suitcase and change out of yesterday's clothes and into a pair of capri jeggings and a cute top. I opt for practical shoes.

"I'm going to see Maxim," I declare. I don't care if I have to walk across Chicago, I will get there, and I will see him

I ignore my mother's dire warnings and protests and leave the building. It takes me all afternoon to get to the Kremlin on public transit.

The moment I walk through the front doors, the guard shakes his head. "Get out. You and your mother are forbidden from entering."

"Please, I just need to speak with my husband."

"Get out, or I throw you out. I'm on strict orders," he tells me. "If you come back, I'll call the police. And you wouldn't want that, would you? Aren't you supposed to be dead?"

And that's when it hits me. I definitely don't want to be dead.

And if I'm not dead, then Maxim has control of my money. Which means his obligation to Igor will still be in place. Unless he believes I nullified it.

Either way, it's a good place to start. I nod. "Please call the police. I want to report myself not dead."

Maxim

I'M on the couch working on drinking myself into oblivion again when my phone rings. It's the security guard downstairs.

"Fuck off," I mutter and dont answer.

He calls Ravil next.

"Huh. Well, call her bluff. Call the police on her," Ravil says.

My head snaps up. "You've gotta be shitting me."

Ravil shrugs. "She says she's going to report herself undead unless you come down."

I settle back and nod. "Call her bluff. She has to stay dead if she wants to control her money."

"I was going to wait a few days to tell you this, but—" Nikolai starts.

I hurl my glass at his head. It misses but smashes against the wall, shattering.

"Right. I'll wait a few days." Nikolai has the grace to look unaffected by my attempted assault.

It shouldn't be so hard to go one day without hearing her goddamn name.

Without thinking about her. Imagining I smell her. Wondering how I could be so stupid as to get played.

Forty minutes later, the asshole guard calls again. This time I answer, ready to chop off his fucking head. "What is it?" I snarl.

"The cops want to talk to you."

"What?" Fuck. She actually went through with it.

I don't want to admit what that does to me. She just gave her fortune back to me. But I can't do this. I don't know what kind of game she's playing, but I won't let her play me again. No fucking way.

"Yeah, I think you might be a suspect in the bombing," the guard says in Russian.

Ah. Now I see her angle. Or do I? Fuck, I have no clue. I can't think straight.

I'm supposed to be the Fixer, but I can't fix a goddamn thing right now.

I head for the elevator, and Ravil, Nikolai and Pavel get in with me. At least I know they'll always have my back.

Brothers you can trust.

Just not women.

I go downstairs, and there's two cops in the lobby standing with Sasha and the guard.

"Here he is." Sasha gives a big smile and a wave. "You see? I'm not hiding from him."

The female police officer narrows her eyes. "So you went into hiding after the explosion, and your husband thought you were dead? But now you're not hiding from him?"

"I was never hiding from him. I was trying to protect him from trouble. My father was the head of the Russian *mafiya,* and after he died, I feared some of his men came after me for revenge."

"Russian *mafiya,*" the male police officer repeats, looking us all up and down suspiciously. "What men were these?"

Sasha shrugs. "I don't know."

"How long have you known your wife was alive?" the female officer asks me.

"Since last night." No point in lying.

"And you didn't bother to notify us? Neither of you did?"

"Like I said, I was laying low. In case they were after me." Sasha has the nerve to walk over and stand beside me like we're a unit. She wraps an arm around me.

If it weren't for the police, I would shove her away. Except I feel her trembling.

Aw, fuck.

I don't want to care about that.

I don't want to even have to try to figure out what my conniving devil of a wife is up to right now.

Is she trembling over me or over the cops?

Gah.

I grab her by the nape and yank her roughly around to kiss her hard on the mouth. Then I lift my head and look pointedly at the cops. "I'm so happy she's alive."

I wish she wasn't breathless, looking up at me like she's never going to look away.

It takes some more back and forth, and the promise of a

detective following up, but the damn cops finally leave. I walk Sasha around the corner, where I pin her to the wall by the throat. "I don't know what your game is now, *caxapok*, but you can stop playing it. It's over between us."

Her eyes fill with tears, and I muster every bit of rage I have against her to keep those glittering drops from moving me.

"Maxim, please. I just want to tell you what happened."

I tighten my grip on her throat, just enough to shut her up. "I don't want to hear it. I don't want to hear any of it. I don't know what you think you proved by saying you weren't dead, but I won't keep you. Look for the divorce papers. Your mom will still inherit, and that way you don't have to stay dead." I release her and walk away.

I'm barely able to breathe from the pain slicing through my torso, but I don't show it. I'm not going to pass out again and let her see how she ruined me.

It's over between us. I can never fall prey to her wiles again.

CHAPTER 22

*S*asha

"WE SHOULD GO TO RUSSIA," my mother says. It's been two days since I saw Maxim at the Kremlin, and I haven't left the hotel room. I'm sitting by the window looking out at the street below. I alternate sitting here with pacing around the small room.

I don't know if I'm thinking, or I've just shut down.

"No."

"Please, Sasha. Be reasonable. We can't stay here forever. Soon Ravil will figure out the hotel is still charging his credit card, and we'll be kicked out."

"You did this," I snap at her. "You took away the only person who ever really cared about me!"

My mother's eyes widen. "What are you saying? I'm the only one who ever really cared about you."

"No." I'm so sick of the hot tears that keep leaking from my eyes. "Maxim really cared. He listened. He supported my dreams. And now he's terribly hurt because he thinks I tried to trick him."

She shakes her head dismissively.

"If you want to leave this hotel, you should help me figure out how to fix this."

"Maxim said he would file for divorce?"

I glare at my mother. She loves that little nugget because it means she'll get my money. "I don't want a divorce. I want Maxim."

My mother sighs. "What about the lawyer?"

"What lawyer?"

"Isn't Ravil's fiancée a lawyer? Maybe she's drawing up the papers. You could go and talk to her."

I blink at my mother. It's not the worst idea.

I don't know if Lucy likes me, but she was certainly kind before. I pick up the phone and call her law firm to book an appointment.

I will make this work. I have to make this work. I'm not going to sit around passively letting people move me around the chess board like a pawn. This is my life, and I have to fight for what I want.

Maxim

I'M at the bar for the third straight night in a row when Pavel plops down beside me on a barstool. He doesn't look at me, just examines the bottles behind the bar with a cool indifference.

The bartender comes over and takes his order for a beer.

He sips it slowly, still not acknowledging me.

"Whatever you want to say, rethink it. I promise I don't want to hear it."

"Hmm."

I pick up my rocks glass and gesture with it. "This time my aim will be better," I threaten.

He says nothing, just takes another pull on his beer.

Fuck this. I throw down a fifty and start to get up from my seat.

"She was fighting with her mother," Pavel offers.

I don't want to stop.

Walk away. Just walk the fuck away.

Goddammit. I sit back down.

"Her mom was saying she should've let her burn."

If Pavel wanted to pick the one thing to make me react, he chose wisely. A wash of cold and then red-hot rage burns through me. "*Excuse me?*"

"They were fighting," he repeats. "I really don't think Sasha had anything to do with the plan. She kept begging me to tell you that. And her mom was telling her she'd done it for her, but Sasha was calling bullshit. She said Galina was basically stealing her money."

My heart flops around in my chest. Indecision makes it hard to breathe. "You're just now telling me this?" I snarl, deciding all of this is now Pavel's fault.

He's wise enough to get off his stool and back away, hands held up in surrender. "I tried."

I shake my head. "No, you didn't."

I may want to never see Sasha again, but the idea of her being in danger from her own mother gets me up and moving fast.

Thank fuck I killed Viktor and Alexei. Would they have killed my bride if she'd tried to leave?

I pull out my phone as I get in my car and call Ravil. "Where are they?" I bark into the phone.

He waits a beat before answering, showing me he's still top dog. When he speaks, his voice is smooth as caramel. "I presume you mean Sasha and Galina?"

"Yes. I assume you're keeping tabs on them?"

"They're still in the hotel where I left them. Their tickets to Russia, booked under false names, went unused."

"What hotel?"

"You should just come back here."

"Don't fucking tell me to come back there."

"No, really, come back. If you're looking for Sasha... she found a way in."

It takes me several moments to think that through. Nothing gets by Ravil, he's our *pakhan*. No one can make him do anything except...

"Lucy let her in." I surmise.

"She's in your room."

My heartbeat calms. She's in my room.

Safe.

No one can touch her there.

No one but me.

I'm still torn. Not sure what to believe. But Pavel's report ties in with what she tried to tell me. And her actions. She didn't stay dead. She hasn't left the country.

I step on the gas, screeching into the parking garage below the Kremlin and taking the private elevator to the penthouse.

I stalk into the suite without a word to anyone, rolling my shirtsleeves up as I go. As if I'm about to take care of my errant wife with a good old-fashioned spanking.

Which... actually sounds fun.

Some of the weight that's been crushing my chest since I

thought she was dead lifts. I push open the door, then step inside and quickly close it when I see what's waiting for me.

Sasha's naked in the middle of the bed. Naked except for a pair of red stilettos. Apart from the shoes, she's the spitting image of the picture she'd made six years ago when I'd found her in my yacht cabin, offering herself up to me on a platter.

I don't like the scene. I didn't like it then, and I like it even less now. It feels like another manipulation. But then I notice how unsure she looks. It's that, more than anything, that breaks down my resistance.

I lean my back against the door and scrub a hand across my face. "What are you doing?"

She swallows. I don't like to see her so nervous. "I left my heels on," she offers. "For punishment."

The fact that she's thinking the same thing I was when I came in busts down even more resistance. But I don't want to think with my dick here. I can't let her fool me if this is another trick.

"No tricks," she promises, reading my mind. Without trying to look sexy, she scoots off the edge of the bed and then shocks the hell out of me by dropping to her knees in front of me. Her fingers reach up like she's going to unbutton my pants, but then seems to think better of it, and they flutter back down.

We're not there yet.

She holds her hands together in her lap, instead, gazing up with those brilliant blue eyes. "I'm not playing you. I wasn't then. I'm not now." Tears shimmer and release, falling down her cheeks.

My resistance gets blown to smithereens.

"I'm here to give myself to you. Because my heart and body and soul belong to you. They always have."

"Sasha," I choke and drop to my knees in front of her. I

lean my forehead against hers and cup the back of her head. "Sasha… you broke my heart," I admit.

She holds back a sob, her bare belly fluttering. "You're breaking mine."

Aw, fuck.

"Maxim, I got out of the car before it blew up because my mom opened my door and told me to... I didn't know their plan in advance. I wasn't part of it. I don't want to be dead to you—or divorced. Please believe me."

"Sasha," I croak. I'm broken now. Completely broken. Utterly demolished. Sasha tore me apart and left me gasping for breath on that sidewalk and in that hotel room.

I stroke her hair.

"My mom just cared about the money." Her voice breaks.

"I know," I admit.

"She tried to tell me you were planning to kill me, but she was the one with the plans."

I thumb the tears away, but they keep falling.

"You're the only person who ever cared about me. I can't lose you, Maxim. Please."

"You have me," I say quickly before she begs more. "You'll always have me. I'm sorry I didn't believe you."

I claim her mouth with the kiss to end all kisses. Searingly passionate. Ravenous. Possessive. I need this woman like I need oxygen. "I'm sorry, sugar," I rasp against her lips. "I should have trusted you. I should have trusted you back then, and I should have trusted you now. I just—"

"I know. Your mom did a number on you. You think women manipulate. I promise I'll never trick you. Not ever."

Hearing my deepest wound spoken aloud by my bride—hearing it understood, held in compassion, does something crazy to me.

All the devastation Sasha wrought on my heart suddenly

seems worth it. To be remade this way. With trust between us. With this vulnerability and allowance.

"Sasha, forgive me," I choke. Now I'm the one begging. "I'm sorry I didn't believe you. I *know* you. I should have hung onto that. I know the heart of you. Who you are beneath all the posturing. You're sweet, and caring and kind. You lift and take care of everyone around you. And, *caxapok*, I consider taking care of you to be the biggest honor ever bestowed on me. My debt to Igor will never end."

"Maxim." Sasha breaks down completely, covering her mouth to hide her sobs.

"Come here, beautiful." I help her up and kiss her again, pushing her onto her back on the bed.

I go slowly. Like tonight's our wedding night, and she's the virgin who waited all these years for me. I kiss from her jaw down her throat. Between her breasts. I squeeze one breast roughly as lust kicks impatiently through my veins, but I force myself to take my time, sucking one nipple into my mouth while I squeeze and massage the breast. "My beautiful wife." I murmur, switching to the other nipple. I squeeze and pinch the first nipple as I suck the second one.

Sasha's sobs have calmed, and she moans, thrusting her glorious breasts in the air. I kiss between her breasts and down her belly, flicking my tongue occasionally to make her gasp. I skip her sex, working around one hip and down her inner thigh.

Her legs and belly tremble.

"Let's see that pretty pussy of yours." I push her knees wide and just stare, drinking in the sight of her pink, glistening flesh. "You're always so wet for me, aren't you, sugar?" I barely brush my thumb over her clit, and she jerks and shivers.

"Y-yes."

"You saved yourself for me." I'm a fool, but I want to hear it. That she saved herself for me not because Igor told her to.

"Yes," she admits. "I always wanted it to be you."

I lick into her, parting her labia with my tongue, tracing around the inside.

She clamps her knees around my ears.

"Naughty girl." I give her pussy a little spank. "Keep those knees wide for me."

"Oh," she moans.

I apply my tongue with a little more vigor, sucking on her nether lips, nipping. I push her clitoral hood back to get my lips around her little nubbin.

Her hands fly to my head, and she pulls at my hair.

I suck harder and sink my thumb into her channel, pumping it in and out.

"Please, Maxim. I need you." She pulls my hair, trying to tug my mouth off her.

"You need my cock?"

I've never had a woman look at me the way she does now. Like I'm her entire world. Like the sun rises and sets by my word. She nods, never taking her gaze from it's lock with mine.

"Please," she begs again.

Well, who the fuck am I to deny my bride anything?

I step off the bed to strip out of my clothes and then climb over her. I don't want to wear a condom. I want to claim her completely—put babies in that belly of hers and keep her on her back for the rest of her days, but I know it's not right. She has career dreams that she's just getting started on. We have plenty of time for a family later. If that's what she wants.

I roll a condom on and line myself up with her entrance. "I love you," I say as I push in.

She gasps and tears up. "I love you, Max." She grabs my hips and pulls me in deeper, wrapping her legs around my back.

I lean down and bite her ear as I slowly rock into her, trying to hold back from pounding like a fiend.

"I need you," she weeps. "I want this. With you. Forever."

I grin, thrusting in a little harder. "Good thing I've already got you locked down, then."

A relieved laugh tumbles out of her. "Will you marry me again? I want to do it over. For real."

My heart squeezes. Of course she wants that. My good girl who kept her innocence for the man she married. She was denied the white dress and flowers. The celebration. All she had was a funeral, a forced union, and dick of a husband who threw her over his shoulder and carried her off to the airport.

I slow my thrusts to lean down and take her lips tenderly, sipping from them. Exploring their softness. "Sasha, will you do me the honor of marrying me?"

"Yes." She laugh-cries.

"Let's have a destination wedding," I say. "We can fly all your friends to Bali or something."

"Yes, yes, yes!" she exclaims. "I love that."

I smile down at her, and she's so radiant it hurts. My control slips. I brace my hands on either side of her head, bracing her shoulders as I thrust in deeper and harder.

She rocks her hips to meet mine like she's eager for even more.

"Who's going to make you scream when you come, sugar?"

"You are," she gasps. "Maxim. My husband."

"Blyat." I lose my head, slamming into her with enough force to rock the bed against the wall.

221

She receives me—moaning louder and louder, urging me on until we both shout out our releases at the exact same moment.

I shower her with a hundred kisses, cover her beautiful face with them, her neck, her ears, her forehead. Then I drop all my weight on her to blanket her completely.

"Oof," she laughs.

I roll us both to our sides, staying inside her.

"Maxim…" Sasha sounds serious again.

I stroke her hair back from her face and cradle her cheek. "What is it, *caxapok*?"

"What are you going to do with my mother?"

I immediately understand her anxiety. "I'll take care of her, Sasha," I promise. "I mean, I don't plan to invite her here to live with us, but…"

"Right." Sasha gives a relieved laugh.

"Maybe we should split your inheritance—give your mom half. That way she won't be acting out of powerlessness and desperation. How do you feel about that?"

"Wow. Yes. Is that okay with you?"

"I didn't marry you for your money. I've told you that. The question is whether it's okay with you."

"Yes. I love that." She returns the shower of kisses, landing them on my face and tattooed chest. "You're a good man, Maxim. Thank you for your forgiveness."

I cradle her face in both hands. "There's nothing I wouldn't do for you, sugar. Believe that."

CHAPTER 23

I BASK in the euphoria of being in Maxim's arms for a long time.

Eventually, though, hunger and concern for my mom bring me back to reality.

"Does everyone out there hate me?" I snuggle closer to Maxim for protection against my thoughts. I realize I will be living with these guys. Lucy was kind, listening to my story and finally agreeing to bring me here to try to fix things, but I don't know about the rest of them.

Maxim shakes his head. "No. They were all still watching out for you. Ravil knew right where you were, and tonight Pavel fished me out of the bar to advocate for you. He told me about your argument with your mother."

"He did?" That surprises me, considering the indifference he showed at the time.

"If anyone was cruel to you, I'm sorry. It was only

because they are protective of me. I'll make sure it never happens again."

I shake my head. "They were fine. I understand. I kind of want to hide in here forever, but... if I don't get back to the hotel, my mom will think you killed me." I offer a wry smile.

"We can text her."

"I don't have a phone." I manage a lopsided grin as Maxim's brows come down.

"Fuck. I'm sorry, Sasha. I never wanted you to suffer."

"Plus, we should get her out of that dive of a hotel. If you don't mind." I cringe a little, hearing how I might sound like the spoiled brat again. Like I just came here because I was desperate.

But Maxim swings up off the bed. "My bride has spoken."

My pulse quickens at his words, that rush of warmth filling my chest again.

"I want to put babies in you," Maxim announces out of nowhere as he's pulling on his clothing. "Badly."

I go still and stare, my face heating. My clit pulses in response.

"Of course, we'll wait until the timing's right for you."

"I want your babies," I blurt, my flush increasing. "But yes, maybe not quite so soon."

Maxim's smile is warmer than the sun. He buttons his shirt, regarding me. "You might want to put some clothes on before we go."

"Oh." I realize I'm still standing here naked. I retrieve my clothes from the closet where I'd ditched them and get dressed.

Maxim waits for me at the bedroom door, taking my hand and squeezing it before pushing it open. "Don't worry," he murmurs. "I'll always protect you, Sasha."

My smile wobbles, remembering that I almost lost him, but he kisses my forehead, and I tip my face up to catch his lips against mine.

"My wife will be staying with us, after all," Maxim announces to everyone in the living room.

They take it with the same casual grace they welcomed my first arrival.

Dima gives a lazy fist pump and "woot-woot." Oleg nods. Nikolai says, "Welcome back."

"Good. I was counting on Money Bags paying for more cable channels," Pavel deadpans, flipping the channels. "I already ordered them."

Lucy smiles at me from the breakfast bar where she sits eating perogies. Ravil stands close behind her, stroking her swollen belly and pressing his lips to her temple. It's sweet.

Everyone here is sweet. They're easy to get along with. Real. They're my family now, and I love them.

"May I? I'm starving." I walk over and steal a pierogi from the plate that Lucy pushes my way.

"We're going to move Galina somewhere—preferably far, far away. Kidding," Maxim winks at me.

"Oh, yeah. I was thinking about another continent, for sure," I agree.

Ravil turns. "Not Russia."

I swallow. I know my mother made her own bed, but I still don't want to see her killed. "No. Somewhere else."

"Maxim will fix it," Ravil assures me. "That's his job."

I steal a glance at my handsome husband, hardly knowing how I remain standing with the way he makes me knees wobble. He takes my breath away.

"Come on, sugar." He tugs me toward the door. "Let's get this over with. I'll take you both out for food when we move her."

"You don't have to be nice to her," I tell him as he pulls me into the elevator and pins me against the wall.

"I will be. Because she's your mama. But if she ever tries to take you from me again, all bets are off."

I wrap my arms around his waist and lay my head against his chest. "Deal."

EPILOGUE

 asha

MAXIM BRUSHES a lock of hair blowing in my face back then rejoins our hands. We stand on the beach at sunset, reciting our vows.

We asked Nikolai to officiate what I'm calling "our re-wedding." The ceremony isn't real, of course—our paper-work is already filed. Our union legal. But this spoiled princess didn't want to be deprived of planning her own wedding, so here we are—on the beach in Ibiza—catching the end of season parties.

I flew my college friends—including Kimberly, who I couldn't leave out—here to help me celebrate. My mom is here on her best behavior, pretending—like me—that this is my first and real wedding.

Ravil and Lucy couldn't travel because it's too close to their baby's due date, but everyone else from the penthouse suite is here—Dima, Nikolai, Oleg, and Pavel, whose lip

227

RENEE ROSE

keeps curling when he looks at my college friends. I guess they're not his type.

Turns out his type is the kinky one-and-done kind, with pre-negotiated scenes involving whips and chains. I guess after he heard about the BDSM club where Ravil and Lucy met, he got interested in taking his sadistic tendencies to the bedroom. I noticed Kayla eyeing him with interest when we first arrived, but I quickly put that idea to bed.

Maxim looks as devastatingly handsome as ever in a crisp white button-down, open at the throat, the long sleeves rolled up to reveal his tattooed forearms.

"Even though you're already married," Nikolai announces in mock formal tones, "I now pronounce you husband and wife!"

My friends cheer and toss rose petals into the air and all over us. Water laps over our bare feet, carrying the petals out to the sea. I jump onto Maxim, straddling him in my short wedding dress as he spins me around and around, kissing me to the deafening cheers.

"Keep going, I'm taking a video," Kayla calls.

Maxim gets too far out to see and a wave splashes up his legs. I shriek and giggle, climbing higher in his arms.

"I've got you, sugar."

"I know." I smile at him. Because he does have me. He always has me, and I love him to pieces for it.

He carries me back up the shore to the dry sand and sets me down.

Nikolai and Dima both pop the corks on bottles of expensive champagne, which they pass around for us each to take a pull from.

"*Gorko!*" Nikolai shouts, in Russian tradition, and Maxim and I kiss, according to custom.

The guys start counting out loud, timing our kiss, which

supposedly proves the longevity of our love, and at the same time, gesture to my friends—unfamiliar with Russian wedding traditions—to chug the rest of the champagne.

My lips stretch into a smile where they are permanently glued against Maxim's.

"All right, all right, enough!" Pavel grumbles after they reach sixty. "We already know you two can go at it twenty-four seven. We don't need the public demonstration."

"Come," you have to smash the glasses," my mother says, producing a pair of crystal glasses out of her bag and handing one to each of us. We move the party up to the paved patio of the enormous beach house Maxim booked.

I pull my elbow back, glancing at Maxim for the go-ahead. He lifts his glass and nods, and we both smash the crystal with as much force as possible for luck.

"Now steal the bride," my mother urges my friends, making shooing motions with her hands. "Make Maxim pay ransom to get her back."

Laughing, my friends grab my hands and dash upstairs with me.

"You always did know how to throw a party," Ashley says when we all scramble onto the king bed together.

"I'm not sure hiding her in my bedroom is really the point," Maxim calls through the door. "But I'm happy to pay."

Kayla snaps another photo of me using my cell phone. It dings, signifying a new email came in, now that it's connected to wifi again.

Seeing the preview of who it's from on the screen, I gasp and snatch the phone out of her hand.

"What is it?" Kayla asks.

"It's from the theater director in Chicago. The guy I just

auditioned for." I hold my breath as my fingers fly across my screen to get the thing open. I squeal.

"What? What is it? You got the part?" all my friends ask at once.

"What's happening?" Maxim asks from the other side of the door.

I rush to the door and throw it open. "I did it!" I shriek, jumping back into his arms. "I'm going to play Anna Karenina!"

A chorus of "Oh my God!" and "That's great!" and "Congratulations!" showers down over me. Maxim bumps me into the air and catches me again, like I weigh nothing.

As if I needed this day to be even more perfect.

Happy tears spill from my eyes.

My mom and the guys push into the room behind Maxim to find out what all the commotion is about.

"This is the happiest day of my life," I sob, dropping my lips to the top of Maxim's head. "I love you all so much. I'm so happy."

Maxim rotates, still holding me straddled around his waist. It's a slow dance, with an audience of everyone I care about in the world.

"I love you," I murmur against his skin. "I love our life."

"I love our life, too." He drops kisses on my arms. "I love you so much, sugar." And then he turns to face our audience. "Now everyone out," he says firmly.

There's a chorus of laughter and protests.

"Lame!"

"The party was just getting started!"

"You keep partying. We have some partying of our own to do here," Maxim says, angling me toward the bed, his eyes dark with promise.

"Yes, please," I whisper as our friends and family exit the bedroom.

Maxim carefully lays me on my back in the center of the bed. "I definitely need a redo on my wedding night," he teases, and I cringe, remembering how I'd escaped as quickly as I could to my apartment, wanting nothing to do with him.

"I saved myself for you," I remind him.

"You did," he says with so much love in his expression.

So much I feel like my heart will burst. I pull him down to me and mate my mouth with his, my tongue licking between his lips, eager for our consummation. Re-consummation. Whatever.

I work the buttons to Maxim's shirt open as our lips twist and tangle. He finds the side zipper to my strapless white mini-dress and tugs it down. I lift my ass for him to pull the dress off. He sits back a moment and bites his knuckle, drinking in the sight of me, naked, except for a tiny white G-string.

"Every time I get you naked, I have to remind myself that this is real. You're my wife. You really belong in my bed this time. I'm not going to get my dick cut off for getting caught with you."

I hook my own thumbs in the waistband of the G-string and shimmy out of it. "All yours, husband. What are you going to do with me?"

His grin is devilish. He shucks his open shirt and then his pants and boxer briefs. "I have about one hundred ideas. Let's get started…"

THANK you for reading *The Fixer.* If you enjoyed it, I would so appreciate your review—they make a huge difference for indie authors.

Be sure to read Pavel and Kayla's short story in *Black Light: Roulette Rematch* and get ready for Oleg and Story's romance in *The Enforcer.*

WANT MORE?

Read the next book in the *Chicago Bratva* series, *The Enforcer*.

MY ATTENTION COULD GET HER KILLED.

I'm damaged beyond repair--brutally modified so I can never reveal what I saw.

Then I spent eight years in a Siberian prison.

In the two since I've been out, I've found nothing to care about.

Nothing except her. She's my weakness. My obsession.

When my past catches up to me, she becomes a target.

I have to capture her to keep her safe. Hold her prisoner until things blow over.

I was already a borderline stalker, showing up every week to watch her play.

She'll never forgive me now--especially because I can't explain.

But there's only one reason I'm still alive: I can't talk.

And I know if I try, everyone I care about will pay the price.

WANT FREE RENEE ROSE BOOKS?

Go to http://subscribepage.com/alphastemp to sign up for Renee Rose's newsletter and receive a free copy of *Alpha's Temptation, Theirs to Protect, Owned by the Marine, Theirs to Punish, The Alpha's Punishment, Disobedience at the Dressmaker's* and *Her Billionaire Boss*. In addition to the free stories, you will also get special pricing, exclusive previews and news of new releases.

Fire Daddy

Hollywood Daddy

Stepbrother Daddy

Master Me Series

Her Royal Master

Her Russian Master

Her Marine Master

Yes, Doctor

Double Doms Series

Theirs to Punish

Theirs to Protect

Holiday Feel-Good

Scoring with Santa

Saved

Other Contemporary

Black Light: Valentine Roulette

Black Light: Roulette Redux

Black Light: Celebrity Roulette

Black Light: Roulette War

Black Light: Roulette Rematch

Punishing Portia (written as Darling Adams)

The Professor's Girl

Safe in his Arms

Paranormal

Wolf Ranch Series

Rough

Wild

Feral

Savage

Fierce

Ruthless

Wolf Ridge High Series

Alpha Bully

Alpha Knight

Bad Boy Alphas Series

Alpha's Temptation

Alpha's Danger

Alpha's Prize

Alpha's Challenge

Alpha's Obsession

Alpha's Desire

Alpha's War

Alpha's Mission

Alpha's Bane

Alpha's Secret

Alpha's Prey

Alpha's Sun

Alpha's Moon

Midnight Doms

Alpha's Blood

His Captive Mortal

Alpha Doms Series

The Alpha's Hunger

The Alpha's Promise

The Alpha's Punishment

Other Paranormal

The Winter Storm: An Ever After Chronicle

Sci-Fi

Zandian Masters Series

His Human Slave

His Human Prisoner

Training His Human

His Human Rebel

His Human Vessel

His Mate and Master

Zandian Pet

Their Zandian Mate

His Human Possession

Zandian Brides

Night of the Zandians

Bought by the Zandians

Mastered by the Zandians

Zandian Lights

Kept by the Zandian

Claimed by the Zandian

Stolen by the Zandian

Other Sci-Fi

The Hand of Vengeance

Her Alien Masters

Regency

The Darlington Incident

Humbled

The Reddington Scandal

The Westerfield Affair

Pleasing the Colonel

Western

His Little Lapis

The Devil of Whiskey Row

The Outlaw's Bride

Medieval

Mercenary

Medieval Discipline

Lords and Ladies

The Knight's Prisoner

Betrothed

Held for Ransom

The Knight's Seduction

The Conquered Brides (5 book box set)

Renaissance

Renaissance Discipline

ABOUT RENEE ROSE

USA TODAY BESTSELLING AUTHOR RENEE ROSE
loves a dominant, dirty-talking alpha hero! She's sold over a
million copies of steamy romance with varying levels of kink.
Her books have been featured in USA Today's *Happily Ever
After* and *Popsugar*. Named Eroticon USA's Next Top Erotic
Author in 2013, she has also won *Spunky and Sassy's*
Favorite Sci-Fi and Anthology author, *The Romance Reviews*
Best Historical Romance, and *has* hit the *USA Today* list
seven times with her Wolf Ranch series and various
anthologies.

Please follow her on:
   Bookbub | Goodreads

Renee loves to connect with readers!
   www.reneeroseromance.com
   reneeroseauthor@gmail.com